Jill's Riding Club

The holidays were approaching and Jill had not planned anything beyond trying some Grade C jumping. And then Ann suggested a riding club. Certainly Chatton needed one and who better than enthusiastic Jill to start it?

Jill's
Riding Club

BY RUBY FERGUSON

Illustrated by

CANEY

London

HODDER AND STOUGHTON

First Published September 1956
Third Impression 1960

MADE AND PRINTED IN GREAT BRITAIN FOR
HODDER AND STOUGHTON LIMITED, LONDON
BY C. TINLING AND CO., LTD., LIVERPOOL, LONDON
AND PRESCOT

Contents

TO

FORM II W.P.S.

CHAPTER I

Who Wants A Riding Club?

IT was one of those wet Saturdays when you argue for a long time about what you are going to do and in the end you do nothing.

"Everybody thinks it would be an awfully good idea if we had a riding club here in Chatton," said my friend Ann Derry.

"Who's everybody?" I said.

"Oh well, everybody, really. And everybody thinks it would be a jolly good thing if you started one."

"I like that!" I said. "Why pick on me?"

"Well, you do more or less start everything round here, don't you?"

"I'm not starting a riding club," I said. "It's too much jolly fag. If anybody else wants to start one I wouldn't mind joining."

"Oh, yes you would," said Ann, with a flash of insight into my character which I can only describe as supersonic. "I can't see you joining a riding club that Susan Pyke started, or that your cousin Cecilia started. You know you wouldn't like any riding club that you hadn't started yourself."

"There's something in that," I said. "What does a riding club do, anyway?"

"Well, everybody joins, and you get a paddock——"

"Where from?"

"Oh gosh, I don't know. Don't interrupt. There

must be millions of paddocks lying around doing nothing. You get one, and you have a meeting once a week or as often as you want, and you get somebody who knows all about equitation to come and lecture to you ; and then you school everybody like mad ; but the point is,

that in the end you can have your own one-day event. Don't you think it would be marvellous to run a gymkhana, for instance, ourselves ? "

I thought this over, and admitted it wouldn't be bad at all.   In fact it appealed to me very much.   It might be worth starting a riding club to run one's own gymkhana, and perhaps it wouldn't be too much of a bind.   Perhaps we could get hold of some worthy types of people who would do the actual work.

" How do we begin ? " I said.

" You mean, you'll really do it ?   Nice work ! " said Ann.

" If we don't like it we can always give it up," I said. " Who do you think would join ? "

" Oh, crowds of people.   You needn't worry about people not wanting to join."

" But we don't want a lot of drips," I said.

Ann thought a bit and said, " I expect we'll have to have *some* drips.   I mean, you can't say ' drips not admitted to the riding club ', because nobody actually thinks that he or she is a drip.   That is only apparent to other people.   I mean, there might be people who thought that you and I were drips."

" Don't be silly," I said.   " You know what drips are. There are two types ; people who can't ride and won't bother to improve, and people who can't ride and think they can.   I don't know which are worse.   You can't teach either lot anything."

" You might be able to do something with the first lot."

" I'd rather not do anything with either lot," I said. " But from what I know about riding clubs—which isn't much—you've got to put up with anybody who wants to join.   You get an awfully mixed entry."

" That's the whole point, I suppose," said Ann. " People join riding clubs to learn as well as have fun. But if you're a properly organised riding club, really important experts are willing to come and teach you because they think they are doing something noble for the cause of equitation."

" I think you'd better run this show yourself if you know so much about it," I said.

" Oh no, Jill, you do it, and I'll back you up."

" That's what you think," I said.

We didn't talk any more about the idea of the riding club, as at that moment Mummy came in and said she would take us to the pictures, seeing it was such a beastly wet Saturday afternoon ; but during the evening I thought the idea over.

If you have read my previous books you will realise that I had done quite a lot since I came to live in Chatton five years ago, in fact there seemed to be very little in the local world of equitation that I hadn't had a stab at at one time or another. My adventures, in fact, had already made four books, and I didn't think there was much else that could happen to me. I had one more year at school ahead of me, and that would be mainly marred by swotting for my leaving certificate, after which I had a wild and woolly dream of going to work as a groom at Captain Cholly-Sawcutt's stables—if he thought I was good enough. I hadn't planned anything for the approaching holidays, beyond trying to win a spot of Grade C jumping—if anybody would be rash enough to lend me a horse to do it on—and I thought it would just be the usual round of events. And now Ann had to crash in with this Riding Club idea.

The one thing I hadn't thought of was a riding club, and I could see that it would be quite something for Chatton to have one. Everybody rode, of course. They learned at various riding schools, or taught themselves, or ' grew up on a horse ' like farmers' children, or were taught by their adoring but occasionally misguided parents who had themselves learned to ride in the dark bygone ages of about 1932. The only time all these people had the chance to meet one another and ex-

change ideas was in the show ring, where as you know
—what with having the needle and thinking how much
better turned out everybody looks than yourself—you
haven't much time for exchanging anything at all but
nervous glances.

So the more I thought about a riding club the more it
seemed to be a useful thing, as well as good fun ; only I
still kept thinking, why pick on me to run it ?   Now if
somebody like Susan Pyke had chosen to run a riding
club I could have understood it—except that I couldn't
imagine anybody in their senses joining a riding club
run by Susan Pyke.   But there were also jolly decent
people like the Heath twins.   Why couldn't they start a
riding club ?   Oh well, I thought, if it's got to be me,
then it's got to be me, and that's all there is to it.
Probably nobody will join and it'll all fizzle out, but
nobody in Chatton can say we didn't try a riding club
while we had the chance.

So the next morning I rang Ann up, and the minute
I heard her answer, " Chatton 92 "—because all the
Derry family answer the telephone in this correct and
proper way instead of the usual Hullo—I said, " How
do you start a riding club, anyway ? "   Immediately I
realised I had got the wrong person, as instead of Ann's
voice I heard Mrs. Derry's rather nervous and milk-
chocolaty one saying, " Oh dear, is that you, Jill ?
What on earth are you going to start now ? "   I felt
like saying, " Measles ", but I said, "Please can I speak
to Ann ? "

I heard her say to Ann, " It's Jill, for you, and I don't
know what she's talking about."

I said to Ann, " You'd better come round here," and
she said she would.   Mrs. Derry, Ann's mother, lives in

a perpetual state of thinking there is going to be a disaster, and it isn't much good having anybody like that hovering around when you are planning to do anything.

In the end we went to our orchard and sprawled under the trees, and my ponies Black Boy and Rapide nuzzled us and tried to chew our hair, and it was all very pleasant, especially as Ann had brought some chocolate.

" About this riding club," I said.   " How would we start it ?   I don't mean to say I'm going on with the idea, but one might as well know."

Ann said the thing to do was to tell everybody at school to tell everybody who was interested, and get them to come to a meeting.

" Where do we have the meeting ? " I said.

" We can have it at our house on Wednesday, because Mummy's going to London for the day."

" Couldn't we have it here in our orchard ? " I said, but Ann thought an orchard wasn't a very dignified or impressive place to have a meeting and we might find that we suddenly wanted to be dignified and impressive. So we decided to have it at her house.

Then before the riding club was even started we began to plan all the things we could do.   Schooling and jumping in the paddock, and games and competitions, and perhaps cross country riding.   Perhaps somebody with horsy instincts and large grounds might be interested and invite the club for a field day and tea.   And then of course we would be able to run a gymkhana.

Ann said, we'd have to have some rules ; and I said, why not let all that kind of thing work itself out as we got to it ?   I felt a few qualms about having rules, because if you have rules you have got to enforce them or it is chaos, and really only a grown-up can enforce rules.

As there would be a number of people in the club my
own age or older I could see nothing but endless argu-
ments if anybody tried to lay down the law, so I thought
it was the best thing to deal with details as they cropped
up and not make regular rules to be fought over.   Ann
said she thought I was a mass of brains and ought to go
into the Diplomatic.

" You could get round it," she said, " by not having
anybody as old or experienced as us in the club, but then
it would be a kids' affair and there wouldn't be any
competition for us."

I agreed that we wanted competition and people or
our own age or older, because the riding club wouldn't
be any fun if it just meant coaching kids.

" And I tell you here and now, Ann," I said, " if I
don't like the way the club is turning out I shall wash it
all up.   The summer holidays are short enough without
fagging about doing things you don't care about doing."

" Leave it all to me," said Ann.   " We'll have a
meeting on Wednesday and see who turns up and how
keen they are.   Other people make a success of riding
clubs and I don't see why we shouldn't.   It's about the
only thing we *haven't* tried in Chatton."

This made me think more than ever that Ann was
better qualified to run this affair than I was, but Mummy
was by now ringing the tea bell and we galloped into the
cottage.

CHAPTER II

A Noisy Meeting

WE didn't mention the riding club during tea, as we both felt it was still on the secret list, but I was getting rather excited about having something definite to do in the holidays and couldn't keep it all to myself, so next morning which was Saturday I said to Mummy, " What do you think is the latest ? I'm going to start a riding club."

" How interesting," she said in a rather cool way. I knew at once that for some reason or other she was taking a dim view.

" What's the matter ? " I said. " I fed the hens."

Mummy said, if I really wanted to know what was the matter, my room was a disgrace, and every single garment I owned wanted darning or hooks putting on or elastic through.

I thought a bit, and then said, " O.K. I suppose I'd better do something about it," and she said that that would be a useful idea, only don't let it interfere with the ponies, which I suppose was justified but rather soul-less of her.

So all the time I was getting my cotton knotted and sewing hooks on upside down, only to tear them off again with muttered oaths, I was thinking about the riding club and wondering who would join. I thought perhaps Ann had been a bit optimistic and nobody would join, in which case we would be back to where we were ; or we might only get a few small kids like Ann's sister Pam, and spend literally millions of glowing summer hours hoisting them on and off their unfortunate ponies, in which case Ann could do it alone.

I then went to the other extreme, and wondered what I would do if a lot of frightfully superior people joined, and expected the riding club to be run in a frightfully superior way, far beyond my humble capacities. This gave me such a jolt that I accidentally sewed the buttons on my white shirt with the same black cotton that I had been using for my navy-blue skirt, but it was dinner time by then and too late to do anything about it.

I went on thinking vaguely about the riding club all through dinner, though in a dim sort of way I realised that Mummy was asking me what sort of bulbs we should get for the garden borders. This sort of thing naturally makes one's parents think one is half-witted.

Meanwhile Ann must have been spreading the news and arousing a lot of what might prove to be misplaced enthusiasm, because when I got to school on Monday morning everybody was pouncing on me at once and asking, " Are you really starting a riding club ? Where is it going to be ? What are you going to do ? Can anybody join ? "

I simply didn't know what to say.

As I was coming out of the Art Room I bashed into Susan Pyke, now quite out of my class and in the sixth form. She looked at me in quite a friendly way and said, " What's this about a riding club ? Good gracious ! You *are* coming on ! "

I said, " Coming on what ? " and she laughed in a sort of tinkly way, and said, " It should be quite fun for the little ones."

This didn't cheer me up; it wasn't my idea of a riding club at all. I found Ann and said, " Something's gone wrong with your publicity. People seem to have got the idea that this riding club is a sort of nursery class. What happens if we get the whole of the junior school turning up on Wednesday, and nobody else ? "

" It'd be jolly noble of us," she said, " to do something for the tinies. We could pat ourselves on the back and feel we were helping the cause of equitation no end."

" I'm not as noble as all that," I said grimly, " especially in the holidays."

So we left it at that, and wondered what would happen on Wednesday.

When I took the ponies their water that night I told them about the riding club. Black Boy hadn't much to say ; he looked at me in a rather gratifying you-know-best kind of way. But Rapide made four different faces at me ; then he gave a very dramatic whinny and blew thoughtfully into the bucket. A lot of water went over my jodhpurs. I told Rapide what I thought of him, but as usual he couldn't care less.

Ann was having spasms of a different nature, wondering what would happen if Mrs. Derry suddenly decided *not* to go to London on Wednesday ; but nothing so awful happened, and she went off early. I decided to ride Rapide to the meeting, so after I had taken the stains out of the knees of my jodhpurs and put on a clean blue shirt I set off. It was a very hot day and Rapide was in a sauntering mood. I suggested that he might trot up the drive to Ann's house so as to look keen if anybody was looking out of the window—as they might well be—but he wasn't having any, in fact he began to do his down-trodden pony act as soon as we got in sight of the house. I was ashamed of him.

I expected to find about six people at the meeting. Instead of that the room was crammed. Quite a lot of the people I had never seen before in my life, but my eye went unfailingly to two points of horror, Clarissa Dandleby and my cousin Cecilia. Nothing could have been worse. Obviously Cecilia was spending the holidays with her friend Clarissa, and if I had known I would have run twenty miles before I'd have started this riding club, only I couldn't know.

I had a cold feeling inside.

" Aren't there a lot of people here ? " Ann said proudly.

" There are only two so far as I'm concerned," I said. " Why on earth did you let them in ? "

" Oh, you mean Clarissa and Cecilia. I couldn't very well turn them away, could I ? I don't know how they heard about the riding club, but they must be keen or they wouldn't have come."

B

" I don't know half the people here," I grumbled, and Ann said, surely that was the whole point of the riding club, to bring strangers together in the cause of equitation.

I said, " You've got an answer for everything."

" Oh, hullo, Jill," said Cecilia, catching my eye. " We've ridden all the way from Clarissa's house for this, so it had better be good."

" It isn't meant for experts," I said, knowing what she was like on a pony at the best of times. " Unless you'd like to give us a lecture. We shall want some people to give us lectures."

" I wouldn't mind," said Cecilia, and my eyes nearly shot out of my head, as what Cecilia knows about riding would go on a postage stamp.

" When you two have done arguing—! " said Ann, coming to my rescue. " Now let's get on with the meeting. I expect you people have come here because you've heard we want to start a riding club these holidays and you must think it's a good idea or you wouldn't have bothered to come. Most of us belong to one or another of the local riding schools, and others are possibly taught by their proud parents or uncles, but the point is we usually never meet except in the show ring. It seems a pity, because I feel that if we could all get together occasionally we could probably teach each other a lot. So the idea is, well—just to get together."

" When I lived at Camberley," said one of the boys, " I belonged to a riding club. We used to have jolly good rallies, and some smashing people came and lectured to us and inspected us. It was terrific."

" I don't know if this will be as terrific as all that," I said. " But the point is that anybody who doesn't like it or think they are getting any good out of it can always buzz off. I don't know how it is, but as soon as I start anything it gets too big before it even starts, if you know what I mean. Our idea was first to get a paddock to hold our rallies, and then to have a rally at least every week in the holidays."

" Where ? " said Clarissa Dandleby. She would !

" I don't know yet," I said. " There must be plenty of paddocks lying around." My one hope was that she wouldn't feel inclined to come ten miles every week, but she dashed my wild hopes to the ground by saying, " Cecilia is staying with me for the whole of the holidays, and we shall be able to come over in the horse box, now we've got a man."

Seeing I was rendered speechless by this idea, Ann said, " The first thing to do is to take the names of all those who think they'd like to join. Stick your hands up, and we'll make a list of the names."

Everybody stuck their hands up, and we started putting their names down. Fortunately there were quite a lot of decent people that we knew, like Diana Bush and the Heaths and other people from school.

" How much is it going to cost ? " asked a third form kid called Brookes.

" I dunno," I said. " I never thought of that."

We thought a bit, and then decided that we'd make it half a crown to be a member, and see how it worked out according to what we had to pay for.

" Don't you think there ought to be an age limit ? " said Cecilia.

Diana Bush said, " Why ? It would be rather nice to have some older people, even twenty-ish ones."

Cecilia gave her a withering look, and said. " What I

meant was, we definitely don't want any kids."

Clarissa said, " Hear, hear. I bar the under-twelves."

I was furious, and wanted to ask who she thought she was to bar anything, but just then Val Heath butted in— and she was the right person to do it, as everybody knew she was jolly good and had won prizes at Richmond Horse Show—and said, " Surely you know that a riding club is meant for all ages, so long as people are keen. Anyone who doesn't like that needn't join. But if any-body of four wants to join they can, and even if they're forty they can join if they want to, though I don't suppose anybody would."

" Hear, hear," somebody said.

" What do we do at the rallies ? " somebody asked. " Just have competitions ? "

" No," said Ann. " We improve the standard of our riding, that's the main thing. We help each other with anything we know. And we get people to come and school us."

" Schooling ! " said Clarissa in tones of utter disgust. " Some of us got past that stage long ago."

" That's what you think," said Val. " No rider ever ought to say a silly thing like that, and you know it."

A boy said, " Even schooling's good fun when you do it together. But I suppose we'll have plenty of games and competitions too. And what about a gymkhana ? "

Everybody shouted out, " Oh, yes, do let's have a gymkhana."

" If we ran our own gymkhana," said another boy, " we could make our own rules, and not have such stuffy judges, like the ones at Lyneham last week who were more or less unconscious all the time and kept rushing off to the refreshment tent instead of looking keen. I do think the least judges can do is to look interested in the competitions."

Another boy said that perhaps the standard of horsemanship at Lyneham had been enough to make any judges unconscious or send them fleeing to the refreshment tent, and as a matter of fact his own uncle often judged at pony shows and wondered why he wasted his time on such a hopeless crowd.

I said, " Look, can't we get back to the point ? We've got to convince our parents and other people that this riding club is going to be a good thing and a useful occupation for the holidays. The first thing they'll ask is, what are our aims and objects."

" Well, what are they, anyway ? " said Cecilia, and somebody else murmured, " Help ! Do we have to have aims and objects ? I thought we were going to enjoy ourselves ? "

" I should say the chief aim and object," said a boy called John Watson, " is to improve the standard of horsemanship in this district. If we tell people that, it ought to fetch them."

" Oh yes—and to promote a spirit of what-do-you-call-it among pony owners," said Diana Bush. " My father says we ought to learn to compete without rivalry. Some people are bad losers, and if we get any of those in the riding club we can knock it out of them. My father says——"

" We might get your father to come and give us a lecture," I said. " If we could get some older horsy people to come and talk to us it would be a help."

" Oh, we don't want to listen to lectures, we can read it all in books," said Cecilia, rather rudely. " And we

haven't decided yet where we're going to hold these
rallies. Perhaps Jill can suggest some place."

"I don't know yet," I said rather miserably. "I
expect something will turn up."

"It's not going to be much good if you haven't got a
field," said Cecilia.

"You shake me to the teeth," I said.

"It would be rather nice if we could get some expert
to come and instruct us in jumping," somebody said.

"There's no reason why we shouldn't. If people
see we are keen they might be glad to help us."

"They might even be glad to give us a field," said
Cecilia sarkily.

"All right, all right," I said. "Aim number one
then ; to improve the standard of horsemanship all
round. Aim two, to work for a gymkhana of our own——"

"Aim three," somebody chimed in. "To have
some fun. I'm sick and tired of hearing about work,
work, work."

"Of course," I said. "Aim three, to have a lot of
fun. Any more aims ? "

"I think we've got more than enough," said Clarissa.

"Enough, anyway," said John Watson, glaring at
Clarissa, "to convince our parents and local experts of
the horse world that we're a keen and sincere riding club.
Everyone in favour, hands up."

Everybody put their hands up, and I said, "To get on
to the next point, what are we going to call the riding
club ? "

"Do we have to call it anything ? " said Ann.

"Well, all good riding clubs have a name," I said ;
and John Watson said, "What about the Chatton
Riding Club ? There isn't another one."

" I don't think we can do that," said Val Heath.
" It sounds so sidey, as if we owned the village.   Couldn't
we have something that suggests a serious aim, like
Perseverance ? "

There was an absolute yell of protest, and somebody
said, " I think we ought to have an imaginative sort of
name.   What about the Pegasus ? "

" I think that name's been used already somewhere,"
said Diana ; and one of the boys said, " Couldn't we go
all western and call it the Buckaroo Riding Club ?   I
think that sounds smashing."

" I should call it the Stinkaroo and have done with
it," said Clarissa crushingly, and Cecilia said, " Oh, you
are a scream ! " and they both went into a fit of giggles.

" Shut up, you two," said Ann.   "What name would
you like for the club, Jill ? "

" Oh, she'll want to call it Jill's Riding Club," said
Cecilia.   *"Cela va sans dire."*

" Quite, quite ! " said John Watson.   " *Avez-vous
trouvez la plume de ma tante ?*   Let's call it La Cecilia
Riding Club."

" You're not a bit funny," said Cecilia, and John said,
" Strangely enough, neither are you."

" I've got an idea," said Val Heath.   " I know where
there's a paddock, if we can get hold of it.   It's on the
Greenlee estate—old Miss Durdon's place—and if she
would let us have the land we could call the club the
Greenlee Club.   It's a pretty name and dignified too."

Everybody agreed that this was a good idea, and Ann
said, " How do we get this business of the paddock fixed
up ?   Would you be able to do that, Val ?   I mean, see
this Miss What's-her-name and ask her if we can use
the land ? "

"Oh gosh, no," said Val. "I was only making the suggestion. Somebody else will have to see about it. My father and Miss Durdon have been having rows over land for about the last forty years. The Heaths and the Durdons have always been at daggers drawn. If she even knew that I was behind this she wouldn't let you have a paddock for untold gold."

"That does sound hopeful !" I said.

"There's no reason why she should know the Heath family are interested," said Val. "One of you ought to go along and see her. I suggest you go, Jill. You've got plenty to say, and you're not terrified of old people."

"Help !" I said. "Is she awful ?"

"She's probably not bad if you approach her the right way. I mean, she's keen on horses—that's a point. And it's a perfectly serious business deal. I don't see why she shouldn't let us have the land. It isn't being used for anything else."

"If we rent it, how are we going to pay for it ?" said Ann. "The half-crown subs. may not be enough."

"What I was thinking," said Val, "was that she might be induced to charge just a nominal rent of about five bob for the eight weeks of the hols. I mean, anybody with horsy instincts ought to be proud to have their land used for a thing like a riding club. In her palmy days she used to ride to hounds, and though she's about a hundred now she must have some decent feelings left about equitation. If I was a rich old woman with land I'd practically go down on my knees and beg people to use it for a riding club. She probably only needs asking."

"All right," I said gallantly. "I'll go and ask her. Only somebody will have to come with me."

" I'll go with you," said Clarissa promptly.

" That's torn it," muttered Ann.

" We'd better vote for who goes with me," I said.

" I'll go," said Diana, " if anybody will vote for me."

I told everybody to put their hands up for Diana, and then for Clarissa, and when we counted the votes were even.

" Right-ho," said Clarissa. " We'll both go."

I looked at Diana, and she put her hand on her heart and rolled her eyes up.

I first met Clarissa at a garden fête which a person called Mrs. Whirtley was getting up ; that is to say, Clarissa and I were both on the committee and went to the meetings. She was sixteen and considered herself a hard woman to hounds, and was always muttering darkly about having ridden in her first point-to-point when she was only eleven, in fact she gave you the impression that she belonged to the higher realms of horsemanship, until you saw her on a pony. How that girl kicked, bounced, and shoved was an eye-opener.

" We'll go and see Miss Durdon tomorrow," said Diana. " That's settled."

" And if she lets you have the paddock," said Val, " couldn't we all meet there on Saturday for the first rally ? "

Everybody agreed that that would be marvellous, and that was actually the end of the meeting, though everybody was by now talking at once, as if getting the paddock from Miss Durdon was a foregone conclusion and all we had to do was to ride round there and enjoy ourselves.

When I got home and thought things over there seemed to be a lot of ' Ifs ' about the riding club. If we

could get the paddock. If we had enough money to
pay what Miss Durdon might ask for it. If the members
were keen enough about the real aims of the club and
didn't just want to play about. Etc. Etc. I felt that
what I needed was some expert advice. I thought I
might go up to the riding school and consult Mrs. Darcy,
but there again the situation was tricky. She might
think she should have been consulted before I called the
meeting, whereas one does like to do things off one's own
bat, a thing no grown-ups can understand.

In the end I went down to the library and asked the
librarian if she had got any books about riding clubs.
She looked at me in a vague sort of way, and I had to
repeat Riding Clubs, about four times.

In the end she said she'd go and see, so she clambered
down from her stool very slowly and doodled away into
the dark recesses of the library where doubtless all the
dull unwanted tomes were kept, and after about ten
minutes she came back and just said, No. I said,
could I go and look myself, and she said I could if I
liked, and if there was anything it would be under Horses
and Cattle on the top shelf in the far bay, but she had
already looked and there wasn't anything. I went myself, and how right she was! Evidently how to run a
riding club was something one had to work out for one's
self by trial and error, with no aid from great literary
minds.

When I got home I rang up Ann and told her about
my lack of success, and asked if among all her pony
books there wasn't one about running a riding club, and
she said there was one, and she'd already gone through
it carefully but it wasn't going to be much use to us.
The children in it had boundless parkland at their dis-

posal and were instructed by their uncle who was a famous equitation expert, and though it made a jolly good story she had chucked it out of the window in exasperation as it wasn't true to life.

I said, " Just think, the world is full of famous literary people and nobody can write a book about how to run a riding club ! "

Ann said, " Don't be silly, there must be dozens if we could find them," and I said bitterly, " Go on then, find them."

Ann said she didn't know what I was worrying about, I had got a lot of keen people and keenness was the only thing that counted. The riding club would practically run itself. I said I hoped she was right.

CHAPTER III

Fuss About A Field

ONE thing we didn't do," said Diana Bush at school next morning, " is to get a President for this riding club. Somebody impressive."
I was dumb and speechless.

" My father would be it," said Val Heath, " though I suppose you'd not think he was impressive. What about asking Miss Durdon ? She'd be flattered. You could ask her to be President first, Jill, and then when she beamed at you and was frightfully pleased you could slip in the bit about the paddock."

I said that I thought Miss Durdon, whom practically nobody had ever heard of, was just about the least impressive person on earth, and Mr. Heath was well known as an equitation expert in the district and I was all in favour of asking him to be President.

" It wouldn't be any earthly," said Val. " The first thing Miss Durdon will ask you is, who is President of the Riding Club—grown-ups are terribly keen on that kind of thing—and if you say the name Heath you certainly won't get the paddock. She'll go up in smoke."

" Oh blow ! " I said. " What *can* I say ? "

" Tell her the committee is considering," said Ann Derry. " That sounds good. Tell her we haven't got round to details yet. Tell her we felt we couldn't do anything about a President until we were sure of a field."

" You think of everything," I said.

The afternoon was a half-holiday and Clarissa was supposed to be meeting Diana and me at the bus stop. We both hoped she wouldn't turn up, but there she was with her specs glittering in the sun, and Diana said, " Galloping goldfish, she's come ! "

Clarissa greeted us in such a friendly way that we were quite overcome. The bus came along and we piled in. When the conductor came round for the fares it turned out that he had once worked as stableman for Clarissa's father. He said, " Well, if it isn't Miss Clarissa ! Been winning any cups lately ? " Clarissa went a coy pink and said, "Well, one can't help picking up a few here and there, though my main interest is hunting." The conductor said he betted there was no woman in the shires faster over timber than Clarissa, and she said it was only right to hold back sometimes, it didn't look sporting to lead the field all the time. By now everybody in the bus was goggle-eyed, listening to this shame-making conversation, and Diana and I could have gone through the floor.

The bus put us down at last at the gates of Greenlee Hall, and Clarissa said, " Well, here we are. Who's going to do the talking ? "

Diana said, " I think you've done enough talking already. All that guff about leading the field ! I should think the huntsman comes out in blisters every time you turn up at a meet. Jill can do the talking. She's got sense."

Clarissa opened her mouth to say something crushing, but I suppose she couldn't think of anything, so she shut it again, and we walked up the drive.

Greenlee Hall was a huge, grey, ugly house with bay windows sticking out all over it, and venetian blinds drawn down in case any sun got inside.

We knocked, and an aged maid opened the door and looked at us as if we were collecting for the guy.

I said, " Can we see Miss Durdon, please ? "

She said, "What name ? " and I said, " The Greenlee Riding Club."

She looked a bit taken back, and Diana gave me a dig and said, " You tactless clot ! "

I realised that I should not have used the name Greenlee right on its owner's doorstep ; however the maid said, " Come in, please, and wipe your feet," which made us feel about six, unless of course she had orders from Miss Durdon to say this to all visitors.

She showed us into the drawing-room which was so dark it took us about five minutes to see anything at all. It was the sort of room that makes you talk in whispers, and it was crammed with little tables and whatnots which were all covered with framed photographs of ancient and grim-looking people.

" There's one photograph of a horse, anyway," said Diana, " but the man mounted on it is practically sitting on its rump, there's room for another one in front of him, and he's got his hands under his chin."

" I see you're admiring the portrait of my Papa," said a voice behind us. " The finest cavalryman that ever threw leg over saddle. That was taken in India in 1898."

I daren't look at the other two, and Clarissa gulped, and said, " How smashing."

I don't know if you are like me and always make a picture in your mind of any new person you are going to meet. Perhaps if so you are cleverer than I am, as I always seem to be wrong. I had pictured Miss Durdon as being about ninety, with snowy hair and wrapped in shawls and wearing a sweet, grandmotherly expression, but actually she wasn't very old at all, and she was rather fat and had ginger hair done in curls on the top of her head. She had on a riding shirt with a mannish collar and tie, and a tough sort of skirt. She had little round bright eyes that looked very shrewd and brisk.

" Now," she said. "What's all this about ? "

I saw Clarissa opening her mouth, and before she could chip in—which I felt would be fatal—I managed to get started on the speech I had made up and learned by heart in the silent watches of the previous night.

" My name is Jill Crewe," I squeaked, " and these are Diana Bush and Clarissa Dandleby. We represent a new riding club which is just being started in Chatton. The fact is, we need a paddock for our rallies, and we thought that as you have a good deal of land you might be able to lend or rent us a bit. We are all very keen and serious, and our objects are good horsemanship and—er—good sportsmanship, which I'm sure you will agree are very important things in life. I hope you will see your way to granting our request."

I thought this was a jolly good speech, and while I was getting it off my chest I could see Diana and Clarissa looking quite stunned with admiration.

I had made it up that Miss Durdon should then reply, " I am very interested in the aims and objects of your riding club, and as I would do anything for the cause of equitation I shall be very glad to lend you free of charge any suitable bit of my land that you would like for a paddock." After which we would all thank her very ardently, which wouldn't be difficult to manage once the spade work was done.

But unfortunately it didn't work out like that.   Miss
Durdon looked at me with her little round eyes and said,
" I suppose you think I'd like to see a lot of children
stampeding round my grounds and tearing up the park ?
I never heard of such a thing.   Absolute nonsense ! "

I was so taken back I was dumb, and Diana said,
" But we are a serious riding club, Miss Durdon, and
we don't tear up ground and stampede," and Clarissa
said. " The bit of land we'd like is at the farthest end of
your park, and you'd not even see us, and this is a business-like request and we are a properly constituted
deputation.   You might like to know," she added,
flashing her specs at Miss Durdon, " that I myself hunt
regularly with the West Morshire, and my father has
been M.F.H."

Actually she couldn't have said anything worse or
more likely to rouse blue murder in the breast of Miss
Durdon, who had always hunted with the Peckhill and
loathed the very name of the West Morshire.

" That rabble of monkeys ! " she said coldly, and
Clarissa was so overcome by hearing her beloved Hunt
called a rabble of monkeys that her specs fell off, and
she was then as blind as a bat and yelled, " Oh, my
specs ! " and started scrabbling about for them on the
carpet, and the next minute she knocked over a little
table and photograph frames came raining down all
over the place.   Diana and I had to shove our fists into
our mouths to keep from screaming with laughter, and
though I was giggling I was nearly sick with disappoint-
ment because everything was going wrong, and now
there didn't seem a chance of us getting any land.

" Clumsy, clumsy, clumsy ! " hissed Miss Durdon,
snatching photograph frames up from the floor.   Diana

and I tried to help her, but the frames wouldn't stand up and Miss Durdon said snappily, " Leave them alone ! "

Clarissa found her specs and put them on, and I said, " Couldn't you really rent us some little bit of land that you're not keen on, Miss Durdon ? I mean, if we go back and tell the others we haven't got a paddock it will mean we can't have a riding club."

" And that will probably mean the end of horsemanship in this district," said Diana, " because if you don't encourage the young entry, what's going to happen when the old ones die off ? "

" Not much fear of that," said Miss Durdon grimly. " Some of us are good for about another thirty years, I hope. I've already told you I don't approve of packs of children on horseback charging round the place without let or hindrance. If they want to ride they should go to a competent instructor at a riding school, like I did. Horsemanship ? Pooh ! You don't know what it is."

" I'm quite sure," said Clarissa, trying to sound haughty and aloof, " that you'll live to regret your decision."

" That's my affair," said Miss Durdon. " I'm not worrying. Good afternoon. If you'll press that bell, girl, the maid will show you out."

There seemed to be no hope left, and yet the saying that the darkest hour is just before the dawn proved true. The door opened and a girl came in. Diana and I let out one yell.

I don't know if you remember in one of my previous books how Diana and I went into the country to visit an aunt of Diana's who had a comic little farm on which

c

she was assisted by a weird girl called Mercy Dulbottle. We had spent an afternoon on the marshes ringing Diana's aunt's ducks, and this girl Mercy proved to be the last word in drips and let the ducks escape as fast as we caught them.

Well, here in the ancestral home of the unspeakable Miss Durdon, at this grim crisis in our careers, who should appear at the drawing-room door looking exactly the same as on that bygone day, but Mercy Dulbottle herself.

She recognised us at once, and said, " Oh, hullo, Diana ! Hullo, Jill ! Have you come to tea ? " She sounded frightfully welcoming, partly I suppose because she hadn't many friends, and partly because it must have been a relief to see anybody human in Miss Durdon's house.

" Oh, hullo, Mercy," I gasped, and Diana said, " Golly, fancy you turning up here. What are you doing here, anyway ? "

Miss Durdon said coldly, " Do you know these people, Mercy ? " and Mercy said, " I should think I jolly well do. How marvellous to see Jill and Diana. Let's have tea at once, can we ? "

This seemed to take the wind out of Miss Durdon's sails to such an extent that before she could speak or act in any hostile manner Mercy had rung the bell and told the maid to bring tea, and was jabbering away to Diana and me as if we were her long-lost sisters. It turned out that Miss Durdon was her godmother, and she simply doted on Mercy and only lived to give her everything she wanted. Mercy had had German measles and had come to stay with Miss Durdon for several weeks to convalesce, and after that Miss Durdon

was going to pay for her to learn farming at an Agri-
cultural College. Personally I thought the Agricul-
tural College would take one look at Mercy and blow
its roof off, but that was neither here nor there.

Miss Durdon was still in a sort of trance, and by the
time she came round the tea was in, and Mercy was
pouring it out and Clarissa was passing round the buns.

" How's the riding these days ? " said Mercy to
Diana, and Diana said, " Well, that's just the point—I
mean——" She stopped and went red, and Mercy said,
" Oh, have I dropped a clanger ? "

" Well, actually," I said, " we've just started a riding
club, only—but it doesn't—it isn't——"

" A riding club ? " said Mercy.   " How smashing !
Could I join, do you think ? "

" No you couldn't," snapped Clarissa.   " We haven't
been able to get a field for the rallies so the whole thing's
off."

" But that's silly," said Mercy.   " Why, Aunt Henrietta has got acres of land doing nothing, and there's a
marvellous little bit down by the west boundary that
would be just the thing for you and your riding club.
I say, what luck you came here ! "

Miss Durdon was by now uttering hollow groans,
what with loathing the sight of us and yet not being able
to deny her darling Mercy anything.

Mercy with blissful blindness then went on enthusi-
astically to tell the wilting Miss Durdon that so far as
riding went practically nobody in England of our age
was as competent as Diana and me.   We were fidgeting
with embarrassment at this flattering untruth, but we
wouldn't have stopped Mercy for the world as she
seemed to be doing our work for us so well, and even

Clarissa managed to push in a bit about how long it took her every Saturday to clean all the cups she had won.

"Think of having these people riding here, in your own paddock ! " said Mercy, as if she was offering Miss Durdon the Crown jewels on a plate.

Miss Durdon made one last effort. " I really don't want them. I don't want to let any of the land. Once they get in the paddock they'll be all over the park."

" That," said Mercy, " would be nicer still." She was the sort of person you simply couldn't flatten ; she had an answer for everything. I just sat there munching currant buns and letting her fight my battles for me.

" You know you're only just beginning to ride, Mercy," said Miss Durdon, " and I don't want to have your seat and style spoiled by a pack of children bouncing about on ponies, when I'm really getting you ready to hunt."

I thought for a minute that Clarissa was going for Miss Durdon tooth and nail, and my heart stood still because if she had let fly at that fell moment all would have been lost for ever, but fortunately Nature took a hand and stuck a crumb right in Clarissa's throat, so she gave a few strangled hysterical coughs and was silent.

" Honestly, Aunt Henrietta," said Mercy, " nothing could spoil me after all your wonderful coaching, and I'm sure it will give you a terrific lift with the Hunt to be entertaining a good riding club on your land. It will look as if you Believed in Young Riders, and the M.F.H. is sure to be very keen on that sort of thing. Do tell Jill it's all settled ! "

Miss Durdon said, " Really, Mercy, I don't know. You shouldn't rush me like this."

" Oh, Aunt Henrietta, be a sport," said Mercy, and Clarissa butted in with, " Oh yes, Miss Durdon, do be a sport ! " while the poor woman half closed her eyes and went green at the thought of anybody who hunted with the hated West Morshire prancing about on *her* land.

I said, " Of course, if we could have the field you could join us, Mercy, and we'd call the club together and have a rally at once."

Mercy said, " Do you hear that, Aunt Henrietta ? I'd simply love to join !   Do say it's all settled ! "

Miss Durdon gave a groan, which might have meant anything at all, and immediately Mercy said, " Oh, thank you a million times ! " and turned to me and said, " There, it's all settled.   When are we going to start ? "

" Oh, thank you, Miss Durdon," I said, and Clarissa and Diana also started saying thank you, Miss Durdon, so she didn't have time to back out of it.

" There's just the matter of the rent," I said.   " I hope it wouldn't cost a lot, as actually we haven't got any money at all—yet."

" Why, it wouldn't cost *anything*," said Mercy.   " The land isn't doing anything, and Aunt Henrietta would be only too glad to lend it to me to amuse myself in the holidays, wouldn't you, Aunt Henrietta ? "

Miss Durdon was by now past speech, but Clarissa said, " It ought to cost something, or we wouldn't feel it was legal, so what about five bob and call it a deal ? "

" Oh yes, that'll do splendidly," said Mercy, " and

we're awfully glad you came, aren't we, Aunt Henrietta ? "

Miss Durdon looked as if she could cheerfully have murdered us, but she couldn't refuse Mercy anything, so she was in what they call a cleft stick, and we'd got the field and it was all too good to be true.

Clarissa, who had rather a legal sort of mind, said we ought to have it all written down, so Mercy brought a piece of writing paper and Clarissa wrote on it, " I, Miss Durdon, declare that the Greenlee Riding Club can have the little paddock on the corner of Bent Lane and Broomstick Lane for their rallies during the holidays for the sum of five shillings.   Yours truly."

" Who said you could call it the Greenlee Riding Club ? " said Miss Durdon in a warlike way.

" It's just to do you the honour," said Diana helpfully.

" Oh, all right," said Miss Durdon.   " But please don't ask me for anything else, Mercy, or you'll bring on my asthma."

She then signed the paper, and Clarissa said Thanks, and put it in her pocket.

CHAPTER IV

The First Rally

IF it hadn't been for Mercy Dulbottle we shouldn't have got the field at all," I explained to Ann as we were on our way to the first grand rally of the Greenlee Riding Club, " so you'd better be decent to her."

" Will that be an effort ? " Ann asked. " What's she like ? "

" At first sight you'll think she's ghastly," I said, " but she's quite a good sort underneath, apart from being slightly mad."

" Can she ride at all ? "

" I wouldn't know," I said. " Actually I think she's a beginner. The only time I ever met her before she was on a bike."

Ann said, perhaps Mercy thought it was a bike-riding club and we both giggled ; however, when we got to the paddock the first person we beheld was Mercy sitting up stiffly on a most beautiful bay hack which I suppose Miss Durdon had lent her or bought for her.

" That's a smashing horse ! " said Ann. " Only I'm surprised Miss Durdon didn't tell Mercy to put her hat on straight."

The field was lovely. It was level and green—about an acre and a half—bordered by a belt of trees on one side and with a low hedge on the road side, and the road itself was merely a lane that very few people used.

You couldn't have imagined a more perfect bit of land
for what we wanted, and I couldn't get over our luck
in having it.

People were turning up all the time, and most of them
I knew ; but there were a few strangers. In the end
there were twenty-seven of us with our ponies, and as
might be expected the crowd was a bit mixed. There
was Clarissa Dandleby and my cousin Cecilia both on

beautiful ponies and very well dressed. There were
also the people that I might call " our crowd ", the
ones from school that I had been riding with for years.
There were a few farmers' children whom I had met in
the show ring. These mostly rode very well, but there
were also some beginners of various ages, and a number
of under-twelves like Ann's sister Pam. Everybody was
standing about looking self-conscious.

" You might begin by telling some of them that it's
usual to come to a rally on a clean pony," said Ann.

" It hasn't rained for a week, and some of those ponies have still got mud on them. It's perfectly disgraceful."

I said, I didn't think it would go down very well if we started off by having a row, and perhaps if we lined the dirty ones up between the clean ones the dirty ones would take the hint.

Nobody seemed as if they knew what to do. I felt a bit awkward myself, but I thought we would have to make some sort of a start. I wished I had a megaphone, even a home-made one, because everybody was talking and there wasn't a chance of making my voice heard.

However there was one person there who had a voice like a ship's siren, and that was Clarissa, and while I was still wondering what to do she charged in and yelled, " Come on, let's get cracking. Everybody line up and face me ! "

" There you are," I said to Ann. " She's going to run the show. I knew it."

" Well, tell her it isn't her show."

" Unfortunately, she's the only one that's got the voice."

But even Clarissa looked stunned when she realised what she had started. The so-called lining-up took about half an hour. There were people there who you would think had never before made a pony stand in line, and there were ponies whose one idea seemed to be *not* to stand in line.

Some of us more experienced ones got down to help the others by pulling and shoving, but as fast as we got two or three into line the first ones were zigging about all over the place. After about another half-hour the line was more or less organised, though it looked like a snake's tail and liable to break up at any minute.

Clarissa looked at me and said. " What do you want done with them now ? "

" Make them ride a circle, I should think," I said.

The chaos that followed had to be seen to be believed, as about nine people started riding round the wrong way, which annoyed the people who were riding correctly. People actually whacked other people's ponies.

" Anti-clockwise, you dopes ! " screamed Clarissa, but that wasn't much good as nobody could remember which way anti-clockwise was and half of them merely turned and began riding the opposite way.

" What a bunch ! " said Clarissa.

" Tell them to stop," I said. " Let's get them sorted out."

So she yelled to them to stop and stand still, and we went round hauling people into position. Needless to say, those who couldn't control their ponies promptly went wrong again. Some went wandering round the field and some merely cropped the grass.

" I give up," said Clarissa. " Why don't you send these nitwits home and have only people who can ride ? "

I said I didn't feel that was fair, and being the first rally people were probably nervous and only wanted encouraging. This wasn't as noble of me as it sounds, because actually I wouldn't have had the nerve to send anybody home, which only shows how unfitted by nature I was to run a riding club.

While I was dithering worse happened, as a boy rode out of the line and said, " I'm fed up with this. I thought we were going to have treasure hunts and things like that." He was a boy called John Watson, a farmer's son whom I had met several times in the show ring. " I didn't come here," he said to Clarissa, " to ride

round and round with a pack of kids." Unfortunately
two or three others heard him and they rode out of line
too. Diana Bush was just behind, and she said, " Oh,
do get back in line. After all, it's the first rally and
we've got to have some sort of drill. It's no good
having treasure hunts until you've got people accustomed
to being called to order."

" Order ! " said John Watson with a snort, but he
saw the force of Diana's remarks and added, " Well,
when you get them in order, or whatever you call it,
tell me and I'll come back."

" Oh for the love of Mike, don't argue, John," I
said, " or we'll never get organised," and Ann added,
" This is what I thought it would be without a grown-up
to give the commands—argue, argue, argue."

John said he wasn't arguing, he was telling us ; but
after a minute he got back into line, and said, " Well,
get on with it."

" We'd better change the drill," said Clarissa.

" What to ? " said John Watson sarcastically.

" I'll tell them to halt," said Clarissa, and then
yelled " Halt ! " at the top of her voice. Of course
about half of the people hadn't the slightest idea how to
halt, and those who did couldn't halt properly because
of the people in front backing into them.

" Let's have a free-for-all canter round the paddock,"
said Ann. " That'll cheer everybody up." This didn't
seem a bad idea, so some of us set off and told the others
to follow on, and it was rather like a chase of wild
Indians, and three people came off, including Mercy
Dulbottle who landed with a whack and made no attempt to get up while her bay went cantering on, trailing
his reins.

"Are you hurt?" I said. "You should get up at once if you're not, and even if you're practically dead you should never let go of the reins."

"I've lost my hat," said Mercy, as if that was the only thing that mattered. And she still sat on the ground.

"Suffering cats!" said Diana Bush, getting down and dragging Mercy to her feet as if she was a sack of turnips. "It's a good thing nobody's watching us."

"But somebody is," said Mercy who had caught sight of her hat in the hedge. "There's a man standing over there, beside my hat!"

"Oh!" said Diana. "It's Major Hooley."

Major Hooley was a retired officer of the Household Cavalry who did a lot of judging at local shows, and was the last person on earth you would wish to see you at your worst. When he saw us looking at him he walked round to the gate and came across to us.

" What's all this ? " he said. " Bedlam in the cattle market ? "

I felt so low at this insulting remark that I got quite mad and said, " We're the Greenlee Riding Club."

" Riding club ? You don't say ? Who's in charge ?"

" Jill," said Ann, pointing at me, and at the same moment Clarissa Dandleby said, " Me."

Major Hooley glared, and said in a very chippy voice, " If there's one thing I can't tolerate it is people not knowing who is supposed to be running a show. No organisation. Very slack indeed. Well, what are we waiting for ? Get along and collect your crowd, and let me see what they can do."

Clarissa and Ann and Diana and I rode round telling people to try and get into line. Everybody made an effort, and soon we were at it again, riding round and round in a rather gloomy sort of ring. Round and round. Round and round. It seemed to be going on for ever. Some people were riding quite well and others so badly I can't describe it. I found myself going into a daze and paying little attention to anything, and before I knew it Rapide had crowded the pony in front, which happened to be ridden by Ann's young sister Pam, who turned round and made a face at me and shouted, " You beast, Jill ! You nearly had me off."

" You ! " roared Major Hooley, pointing at me. " Has anybody ever taught you manners ? "

I felt about six and very humiliated, especially as I caught a glimpse of Clarissa with a mocking grin on her face. I hoped the Major would notice how smartly I collected Rapide, but he wasn't even looking.

My cousin Cecilia was the next to get it in the neck. She was very well mounted on a lovely pony and wasn't riding at all badly, and she had in her hand a silver-mounted hunting crop that she was terribly proud of, and every time she passed the Major she gave this crop a bit of a flourish so he couldn't fail to notice it.

" You ! " he barked, stopping the whole line and striding up to Cecilia. " Where did you get that atrocity ? "

Cecilia looked as if she couldn't believe her ears. " Do you mean my crop ? " she said. " Isn't it a beauty ? "

" Burn it," said Major Hooley. " Do you hear what I say ? Burn it. Schooling with a hunting crop ! Never heard of such a thing."

Cecilia went the colour of a tomato, and I felt almost sorry for her. She collected her pony and went jogging on, but she was biting her lips and I knew she was furious, though of course Major Hooley was perfectly right about the hunting crop.

By now all the ponies had realised the situation and were playing us up in a sickening way. Apart from a few experienced people who wouldn't stand any nonsense, nobody was attempting any sort of control. Everybody looked fed up, and a few had ridden off and gone home.

Major Hooley got us all to a halt, and after clearing his throat, remarked, " So far as I can see, the only person who knows how to sit on a horse is the long girl on the bay hack."

This, believe it or not, was Mercy Dulbottle. Everybody stared at her, she looked terrified, lost both her stirrups, slithered on to the bay's neck and hung there. Major Hooley said, " Give me strength ! "

He then yelled, " Dismount ! " and came up to me

and said, " Well, I suppose you think you're riders ? "

" I don't think anything," I said sulkily. " But most of us *can* ride. It's just that we started off in a muddle and never got out of it."

" Well, that wasn't much good, was it ? " he said. " Did somebody say you were running this show ? "

" I don't know whether anybody did or not," I said. " In the first place it was the general idea. I don't seem to be much good."

" Oh, don't say that," he said. " Just carry on, and I shan't mind giving you a bit of help occasionally."

" That's very decent of you," I said, " but it won't be much good if we're all so rotten."

" You can't expect much at first," he said. " I've seen worse. You've got the raw material and it's up to you to make something of it."

I didn't much like being called Raw Material myself, and as for Clarissa Dandleby she was just about bursting, which amused me a lot.

" What you ought to do," said Major Hooley, " is to get a proper school marked out for next time. A good big one. Then you can fit up your jumps in the middle. Can any of you jump ? "

" Quite a lot of us," I said, " have taken prizes for jumping."

" Well, get them working," he said. " Playing around won't get you anywhere. And when you're a bit more organised I'll come again. You might make quite a decent riding club, even out of this shocking lot."

I could see that everybody round me was writhing under all these insults, but I just said meekly, " O.K. We'll do our best."

" Come along now," he said. " Let's have another

shot at it. Mount, everybody, and we'll try a trot and a canter."

This time things went a bit better, though I wasn't very happy because several people had ridden out and were standing looking on rather superciliously, and I knew there was going to be trouble later.

When we were at the opposite side of the ring from Major Hooley, Ann came up behind me at a beautiful trot and said, " Well, what did you think of that ? I feel as if I was a space ship being hurled through the stratosphere at five thousand miles an hour."

" In one minute from now," I said, " you're going to be barged into by the Neville boy who is coming up on your left side. He looks furious, and I don't feel so good-tempered myself."

Major Hooley yelled, " Canter on ! " and we cantered. Then poor Cecilia, my unfortunate cousin, got it again, as she had quite forgotten the hunting crop episode and was still carrying it.

" I thought I told you to get rid of that thing," said Major Hooley.

Clarissa looked round wildly, and then took him at his word. She hurled the crop away from her as if it was on fire, and it hit John Watson's pony across the hocks and he bolted. We all came to a ragged halt, and watched John's pony careering madly round with John trying to pull him up. At last John managed to slither down and stop the pony expertly. He then walked up to Cecilia and said, " You silly clot ! "

Cecilia said, " Don't be so disgustingly rude."

Major Hooley said, " I think we'll call it a day. Remember what I told you, and I'll look in on you some other time."

He then cleared off, and as I expected everybody began arguing.

Cecilia said, " I propose that this riding club be well and truly washed up."

Ann said it was silly to talk like that just because everybody had got a bit demoralized by Major Hooley's efficiency, and Cecilia said, " I beg your pardon ! Efficient ? The old fool's a hopeless incompetent."

" You know that isn't true," said Diana. " He does know about riding, and he said we had the makings of a riding club."

" He also said we were a shocking lot—— " I began, and Ann said, " I think you're a feeble crowd if you can't stand a bit of criticism."

A girl called Vera Harley said to me, " Well, I'm not bothering to come again, and neither is Mary."

" Oh, don't be so unsporting," I said furiously. " You'll be sorry when we really get things going."

" When ! " said Cecilia with a hollow laugh.

I said in disgust, " Oh, let's go home ! " and then I wished I hadn't said it, because it gave a wrong impression and I hadn't meant to sound feeble.

Clarissa said in her foghorn voice, " Anybody can go home that wants to go home. At least we'll know where we stand then, and get rid of the drips. But there'll be another rally on Monday afternoon. Two o'clock. And it'll be a working party for building jumps. Bring wood and tools and old bedsteads and bracken, and anything you've got in the way of red and white paint and brushes. And you'd better bring some food too, as we'll probably be here till midnight, and anybody who doesn't want to work needn't bother to come."

D

One or two people said, " Good show " and some of those who were hesitating said, all right, they would come. I felt very humiliated, because what Clarissa had said was what I ought to have said myself, only I had been too feeble, and it served me right that she should get the credit for saving the riding club from fading out altogether.

When I got home Mummy said brightly, " Well, how did the riding club go ? Did you have a wonderful time ? "

" No," I said. " It was rotten."

Mummy asked, what went wrong ? So I told her. She said, Well, did I expect everything to be perfect the first time ? If so, I was very silly. I said she just didn't understand, and I went out to the orchard to give Black Boy some apples and tell Rapide that he'd let me down, only he looked so sad I had to give him some apples too. Then I sat down under a tree and read a library book called *The Spy with Eleven Fingers*. only I couldn't stop thinking about the riding club and wondering whether I had better let Clarissa run it after all. I had just got to the bit where the girl agent tries to get out of the country by having herself packed in a trunk and handed over to British Railways for shipment to the Channel Islands, when Mummy called from the back door that there was somebody to see me. I thought it might be Ann or Diana, but it was Mercy Dulbottle.

" I just came along," she said kindly, " thinking you might be feeling dim about the rally."

" So what ? " I said.

" Oh, buck up," she said. " We'll get things going in no time, won't we, Mrs. Crewe ? "

When she had gone Mummy said, " What an awfully nice girl. I've never seen her before, who is she ? "

I said, " Mercy Dulbottle,"—without thinking that Mummy had never before had this peculiar name sprung upon her—and she just said, " Mercy—what ? Oh no ! " and went into a fit of giggles, and I couldn't help starting to giggle too, and by the time we were both helpless with giggling I felt a lot better and decided that I still wanted to go on running the riding club.

CHAPTER V

Treasure Hunt

I STARTED looking round for stuff for making
jumps. There was plenty of brushwood about, but
it occurred to me that that was what other people
would think, and what would happen would be that we
would get enough brushwood to build ten hedges and
probably no timber at all. What we wanted was stiles
and gates, and if we were lucky, some blocks to build
a wall.

I was cantering Black Boy along the grass verge of
the lane and thinking hard when I saw something that
I had often passed before but hadn't really noticed.

This thing was an old gate which had dropped off its

hinges and was lying flat at the entrance to a turnip field. It was probably rotten and no good as a gate, just waiting until the farmer got round to fixing up a new one, but I could see a lot of use in that gate. I knew it was Mr. Trimble's field, and after one brilliant burst of thought such as I get from time to time, I went charging up the lane to the farm.

I was lucky. Mr. Trimble was in the yard.

" That gate ? " he said. " No, it's no use to me. I'm expecting the new one any day now. So you want it for your riding club ? Well, I'm glad it'll be useful as I never like to see anything wasted."

I beamed at him, and he went on, " As a matter of fact, I think there's a drop of white paint lying around somewhere, left over from when Joe painted the garden fence. There isn't much, but it might be enough to give the gate a slosh over."

I said that would be marvellous, and I'd evidently caught him in a most helpful mood, as he said, " Well, Joe has to go down to the station tonight with the flat cart, and he'll be passing your place so he can easily drop the things off for you."

I said, " It's simply wizard of you, Mr. Trimble, and how much will it be ? "

He said, " Oh, that's nothing at all. But I wonder if you'd consider giving my Stanley a few lessons ? I'd pay at the usual rate of course. He's twelve and wants to learn to ride, so if you could start him I'd get him a pony."

I thought it was a case of one good turn deserves another, so I said I'd work Stanley in if Mr. Trimble cared to send him down next morning. I was very bucked up about the gate.

As soon as I got home I rang Ann up and told her. She said, " Well, as a matter of fact, I think the jump-building's off for the moment. I mean, it's wonderful about the gate and it'll be jolly useful later on ; but a lot of people have got very bored with the riding club already, and unless we do something about it they won't come any more, and we shan't have any members."

I said, who told you that ? And she said that practically everybody in Chatton was talking about it, and she didn't know where I'd been not to have heard. I said I thought this riding club was just about the worst thing that had ever happened to me. It was like one of those nightmares you read about in books where people dream they are loaded with chains.

Ann said, " Well, I think we ought to have some fun, such as a treasure hunt, that will attract people and make them think they're going to enjoy themselves, and not just be bashed round in a ring and yelled at by Major Hooley and Clarissa Dandleby."

I said, O.K. we'd have a treasure hunt, if that was what she wanted, and she said she'd start spreading the news round.

As soon as I put down the telephone I started thinking about the treasure hunt, and it seemed to me a good idea.

I went out and leaned on the orchard gate and watched the ponies, doing nothing. It was very soothing. It was a lovely day and gold patches of sunlight were tumbling about in the long orchard grass. Rapide nibbled his foreleg and then tossed his head joyfully ; Black Boy looked at me thoughtfully, knee-deep in daisies. I began to wonder what sort of things we should go hunting for in the treasure hunt.

Just then Mrs. Crosby came to the back door and yelled, " You're wanted on the telephone."

I said, Oh blast, and she said that was no way to talk when it might be to say that my long lost uncle in Australia had died and left me a fortune, as had happened to her sister's son-in-law's mother ; and I said, " Fate ! "—very darkly—and went to the telephone, and it was Clarissa Dandleby.

She said, " I've got an idea. I think we should have a treasure hunt, to make the riding club think it's getting something."

I said, " You're too late. We're having one."

She said, " Oh, nice work. Well, as soon as I've got some ideas worked out I'll let you know."

I said, " Oh, thanks very much, Clarissa, but I've got loads of ideas." Then I rang off and wondered whether it wouldn't have been as well to have a few of Clarissa's ideas to start with, as my own mind was a complete blank.

I drifted into the sitting-room to see if Mummy might have any bright suggestions, and there she was, typing away like mad.

" Don't speak ! " she said, in a sort of squeal.

I stood pawing the ground, and after a minute she stopped typing and said, " There ! It's finished. I've been about three days trying to find the right last sentence, and just when you came in I got it."

From this I gathered that yet another of Mummy's immortal works was ready to go to the publisher.

" What's the last sentence ? " I asked, because I do honestly try to take an interest in Mummy's books though they are not my type at all.

Mummy read out rapturously, " ' As the Golden Doll

tumbled into little Jessica's arms, all her dreams came true.' "

"Gosh, she was lucky!" I said, ironically. "Mummy, do you know anything about getting up a treasure hunt?"

"Oh, are you going to have one? That will be fun."

"That's what you think," I said darkly. "I have my doubts."

"Really, Jill," said Mummy briskly, "I don't know what's the matter with you lately, but whatever it is I don't like it."

"Mostly," I said, "it's coping with people who get me down."

Mummy's eyes flashed, and she said, "I never heard such ridiculous nonsense. You'd better snap out of this dying duck attitude, and realise that nobody on earth can get you down. You let yourself down, that's the only way you get down in this life."

This impressed me, and I said, "Perhaps you're right. Oh, well—Mummy, could you give me some ideas for things we could hunt for in the treasure hunt? It'll be on ponies, of course. And the people are very mixed ages, from sixteen down to about eight."

"So you'll want outdoor things?"

"That's the idea," I said. "I'll write them down. What about a bird's nest? It's all right to take one now because they're all empty."

"Yes—and a horse shoe."

"I pity the farrier!" I said. "They'll all be bombarding him, but it's rather good because he won't have enough for everybody to have one. What about a mushroom?"

"There won't be any mushrooms in early August."

" Oh, yes there will.   There are some in our larder now."

" Is that fair ? " said Mummy.   " I mean, shop ones ? "

" I don't see why not.   Everybody has got a larder at home, and if their mothers haven't bought any mushrooms they'll be unlucky.   So what ? "

Mummy giggled and said, " A brown egg."

" Whizzo," I said.   " What about a white feather ? "

" Better not," said Mummy.   " You'll have all the young ones chasing people's white hens to make them drop a feather.   Make it more difficult.   Say a red feather.   That'll make them think."

I giggled and wrote it down.

In the end the list ran :

A brown egg
A red feather
A mushroom
Ten different wild flowers
A horse-shoe
A birds' nest
A white stone.

The last was very difficult because all the stones round our way are grey.

By now I was really excited about the treasure hunt, and when Ann came round she said she thought the list was very good, and we made about thirty copies on Mummy's typewriter so that everybody could have one. It took us hours to do because of the mistakes.   I kept on putting down the key that says shift, and instead of A Brown Egg I got A Brx$=\frac{5}{8}$ eG$\frac{3}{8}$.   In the end Mummy helped us out, and it was done.

The idea of the treasure hunt had roused the dying

enthusiasm of many, and there was quite a crowd at the rally. Clarissa, who had to have her say, thought the mushroom was feeble, and what about a picture of a famous rider? I had to admit that this was a bright thought, so we altered all the lists with a pencil and gave them out. People said, Help! Oh, Gosh! and How beastly difficult.

My cousin Cecilia said—she would!—"I suppose you'll be staying here, Jill, to do the judging when people come back."

I felt very dim. I hadn't thought, but of course we'd have to have a judge for people to bring their treasures to, but I didn't want it to be me because I was looking forward to the ride and had promised Black Boy a good afternoon's fun.

Just at that moment two mounted figures appeared. They were Mercy Dulbottle and—of all people—Miss Durdon in a high-necked shirt and tight tie and baggy black jodhpurs, looking like something out of the Indian Mutiny.

They rode up, and Miss Durdon said, " I think this treasure hunt is a good idea. Mercy must ride, and if you like I'll stop here and be the judge."

" Oh, that would be simply smashing ! " I said, grinning with relief.

" Don't mention it," said Miss Durdon. " I'll be quite happy here, exercising Westminster Abbey "— which was the peculiar and inappropriate name of her rangy grey hunter.

At the last minute three fat and panting figures arrived on three fat and panting ponies. They were April, May, and June Cholly-Sawcutt, who you will recall if you have read my previous books were the unteachable daughters of the famous show-jumping Captain Cholly-Sawcutt.

This made up the field, and we cantered away. Ann and I were hunting together. First we pelted off to the farrier's to make sure of our horse-shoes, but practically everybody else had the same idea, and after

handing out three—of which Ann and I got one between us—the pestered smith closed his door and told us to clear off. So we dashed up to Mrs. Darcy's place, and luckily one of her ponies had just cast a shoe, and we got it, so we had one each. We were only just in time, as by then half a dozen other people hove in sight and Mrs. Darcy shouted, " It's no good coming here for horse-shoes ! "

The brown egg was easy and we got one each at Mr. Trimble's farm, but then wished we'd left this particular treasure until the end, as we hadn't anywhere to put the eggs except in Ann's saddle bag where they soon came to a sticky end, and we hadn't time by then to get any more.

Then we madly collected wild flowers in Goose Lane. We soon got nine different ones but couldn't find a tenth, and in the end we had to ride to Neshbury Common where we got some sprigs of gorse which we hoped would pass as wild flowers. At any rate they were flowers, and they weren't tame.

I said, " Let's dash home to the cottage. There are two empty sparrow's nests in the orchard, and I can collect my picture of Pat Smythe at the same time. That'll kill two birds with one stone—oh, and you can have that snap of Wilfred White that I took at Chatton Show."

Ann said you couldn't tell it was Wilfred White, and I said, " Well, it is."

We did all that, and also managed to drink a lot of lemonade and give the ponies drinks, which was kind but wasted a lot of time.

" What about this red feather and white stone?" Ann said.

" Gosh ! " I said. " I thought those two up myself. It serves me right."

" If we had any white paint we could get two stones and paint them white," said Ann, " if you think that wouldn't be cheating?"

" There's nothing against painting them," I said. " And I've got the white paint that Mr. Trimble gave me for the gate."

So we got the paint and sloshed it over a couple of stones, but they wouldn't dry and we didn't know what to do with them. In the end we wrapped them up in some newspaper, and most of the white came off, but we shoved them in Ann's saddle bag and hoped for the best.

" My saddle bag's full of burst eggs and white paint," said Ann. " And as for red feathers! What bird were you thinking of, may I ask?"

I admitted that I'd gone a bit too far with this red feather idea.

" If we had some white feathers we could paint them red, if we had some red paint," I said ; and Ann said we hadn't got either, and she already had white paint all over her jodhpurs and she didn't want to turn up looking as if she'd done a murder.

" It was a silly clue," I said. " But I expect everybody else will think so too, and nobody will get any red feathers."

" Well, *we* don't stand much chance," said Ann, " and we've been out two hours already, so we'd better go back. The ride has been fun, at least."

The ride *had* been fun and everybody had enjoyed it. When we got back to the paddock the place was already seething with people, and soon the last of the treasure hunters turned up. They all admitted they'd had a super time, and John Watson said, " Whoever thought of that red feather ought to be made to eat one. I've got everything else but that, but I'm too late back to have any chance of a prize."

Clarissa Dandleby said smugly, " I've got a red feather. It was off a pheasant." But when Miss Durdon, who had sportingly entered into the spirit of the thing, looked at it she decided it wasn't red, it was gold.

Believe me, or believe me not, the whole thing had already been won by June Cholly-Sawcutt who was back half an hour before anybody else and had got everything !

What happened was this. When we all rode off, June, who was only eleven, followed her two sisters who with sisterly callousness rode away and left her, although she kept calling, " Wait for me, you beasts ! "

She was an even worse rider than they were, and soon she found herself all alone. She was fed-up and disappointed, so she gave up the hunt, and turned her pony round and went home, and because she was only a kid she began to cry. She was crying like anything when she rode into their yard and the girl groom, Pansy, said, " What's the matter, June ? "

June told her, and Pansy said, " Well, that's all right. Let's have a look at your list." She read the list, and said, " Come on, June, get cracking. You did right to come home, we've got everything here. I've a brown egg in my hand this minute, and there's a photo of your father in the sitting-room—he's famous enough—so oodle in and get it. There's about a million different kinds of flowers in the hedge along the paddock, and while you're picking those I'll slip up and unpick the red feather out of my beret that I wear on Sundays. There's a horse-shoe hanging on the stable door, and there's an empty birds' nest in the gooseberry bush by the back door, and there's a line of white marble stones that your mother brought from the seaside and put round the rose bed. So what are you waiting for ? "

By now June had brightened up and her eyes were

nearly popping out, so she wiped them and blew her nose and dashed round collecting all the things, and Pansy found a paper carrier-bag to put them in, and she wrapped the egg in tissue paper so that it wouldn't get broken.

June rode peacefully back to the paddock and handed the paper carrier-bag to the astonished Miss Durdon, who said, " There isn't a sign of anybody else yet, and your things are all correct, so it looks as if you've won."

She'd won all right. Most people were short of at least one item, and several people's eggs were broken— including Ann's and mine—and some others had brought all the same kind of wild flowers, such as ten buttercups.

Diana Bush had got a red feather, but she had snipped it off her mother's best hat and it was already broken at the end, and Diana was feeling very dim about what her mother would say.

April and May Cholly-Sawcutt hadn't got half the things, and April had fallen off her pony—she spent most of her life falling off her pony, and would have fallen off a table-top—and hurt her leg, and May was plastered with lime because she had had the bright idea of dipping a stone in a handy lime pit in a builder's yard and had got both her arms in up to the elbows. So June had the satisfaction of saying sucks to her elder sisters.

" What's the prize ? " said John Watson.

I went cold, because I hadn't even thought about the prize, which shows how unfitted I am by nature to run a treasure hunt or anything else, but Miss Durdon said, " The prize is six free lessons in dressage from me."

John Watson said, " Gosh, I wish I'd won," but June —who *had* won—looked completely blank, because far from needing lessons in dressage she had not yet managed to grasp the idea of sitting on a pony properly.

Miss Durdon said, " Ring me up when you want the first lesson," and June said, " Oh. Um. Yes. No. I mean——" And everybody knew she wouldn't.

Miss Durdon, who seemed to have surprisingly and completely altered her character, which had hitherto been grim and non-co-operative, then said, " Now if you'll all come up to the Hall there'll be buns and tea for everybody."

" Well I'm blowed ! " said Ann. " She's read my thoughts. Three cheers for Miss Durdon ! "

Everybody yelled Hip Hip Hurray at the tops of their voices, and Miss Durdon went pink and looked frightfully pleased.

So the treasure hunt finished magnificently, and the whole point of it was that the riding club was now well and truly established, and everybody was keen about it, and I could see we weren't going to have any more trouble. Even Clarissa Dandleby was pleased, and started nattering about " now we'll get down to some real work and fix those jumps," and I went home feeling on top of the world.

CHAPTER VI

Good Hard Work

WE next got down to the jobs of building jumps, tidying up the paddock, pulling thistles, etc., and by now we had a good idea of how many people were going to stick to the riding club and be any use. You know what it is like in anything you are doing, when it gets to a bit of work there are always some people who just ooze off, or have very convenient colds and toothache and the only afternoon the dentist can see them is the afternoon you are doing the work. I hate to sound like a hoary old cynic of ninety, but alas, what I say is true.

However, about eighteen people turned up to work, which wasn't bad. As I thought, we had far too much brush, but some people had brought wood, and my gate was a terrific success. We got two of the young ones to slosh white paint over it. One girl had been crazy enough to bring a lot of gorse. Clarissa said sarcastically, as well she might, " What do you think we're going to do with that ? " and the dim-wit said, " Make jumps," and Clarissa said, " If you want to make yourself into a walking pin-cushion I couldn't care less, but Heaven help the ponies."

We got one lot of people clearing the ground, and another lot pegging out a sort of school, and another lot building jumps ; then when we got browned off with these labours we all switched round.

Suddenly Ann said, " Do you see what I see ? "

I said, " What ? "

" Little Sunshine," she said.

It was Major Hooley. John Watson said, " It only wanted that ! "

Major Hooley walked right over to us and said, " Bit of good work going on here. That's what I like to see, ha-ha."

None of us said anything, as we couldn't think of anything that wasn't either sarky or rude.

" How many jumps do you propose to have ? " said Major Hooley to John, and as John had to say something he said, " We want to have six, but unfortunately it looks as though they're all going to be hedges except for the gate that Jill brought."

" H'm," said Major Hooley. " What height are you making that contrivance ? "

" If it'll stand up," said John, " it's supposed to be three feet. We thought we'd have four at three feet and two at two-foot-six for the younger ones, because in a riding club we think the way you jump is more important than the height you jump."

" Very sensible," said Major Hooley. " I believe in helping those who help themselves, so I've got a lorry coming along with some useful stuff. Ah, here it is."

We couldn't believe our eyes when we saw the stuff that the Major had got for us. There were posts, bars, wood blocks, and even hurdles. It was like one of those dreams where you get everything you want and then wake up and remember you forgot to do your geography homework, only we didn't wake up.

Everybody flocked round the lorry and helped to unload it. It was very exciting. Then Major Hooley took charge. He gave everybody their jobs and he and the lorry-driver went round helping to knock in posts and similar heavy tasks. We built a wall with the woodblocks, and arranged a bar jump with hurdles. We then made a frame for the in-and-out and filled it up with brushwood, and Major Hooley produced a pair of hedge-clippers and trimmed it ; and finally my gate was properly erected and given some very professional-looking wings.

Major Hooley then sent the lorry back to his place to bring whitewash and several brushes, and when they came we started to whitewash everything. The wall, hurdles, and bars were done, and the ring marked out. It looked supersonic. I couldn't believe this good jumping course was really ours, and by now we were all dying to try it.

" All we need now," said Clarissa, " is a triple bar."

" Gosh ! " I said. " Is that all ? You would think of something we haven't got."

Ann nudged me and said, " Don't you think you'd better make a speech to thank Major Hooley ? "

I hadn't any time to think, but I had to say something, so I said, " On behalf of everybody I want to say a terrific thank you to you, Major Hooley. We think this is terrific of you, honestly we do. If it hadn't been for you we shouldn't have had a proper riding club at all."

He looked quite pleased, and said, " Well, I hope you'll make use of the jumps now you've got them," and somebody said, " I vote we all whizz home and get a snack and then come back here and do some jumping."

We all forgot we were aching with weariness and bleeding from a thousand scratches, and we went pelting off home, and then came back for the evening. When we got back we decided that everybody should jump a round in turn. Some of the younger ones said they couldn't possibly do three-foot jumps, so we decided that they could jump the two-foot-six ones twice.

"Jill ought to have first go," said Ann, " because she's running this thing, anyway."

A few mouths opened in surprise, but nobody said anything, so I started off on Rapide.

It was a lovely course, but I felt uncomfortable because it would look awful if I didn't do a clear round.

I cantered Rapide and went for the first jump, which was the two-foot-six hedge. Rapide went over like a bird. He also took the bar without any trouble, but for some unknown reason he refused at the gate and brought it down at the second attempt. He soared over the three foot wall, but hated the sight of the in-and-out and ran round it, and then did the next two-foot-six in great style.

"I think you had about nine faults," said Ann when I got back, and I said, "It was a ghastly exhibition, but after all it was the first time, and I don't think Rapide is cut out to be a pathfinder. Black Boy could have done it on three legs."

Clarissa Dandleby went next on her chestnut pony Havelock. I think she thought she was going to show the world, but Havelock didn't shine either as he even managed to knock down one of the two-foot-six brush fences, and bucked like mad all the way round. Diana Bush's pony refused the wall three times; and then John Watson went in to show us how it ought to be done and created a complete scene of destruction, laying practically everything flat on the ground. We were all laughing so much we could hardly get the jumps put up again, and John said, " I believe there's a hoodoo on this course."

However the first rider after we'd re-erected the jumps did a clear round and said, " Hoodoo, my foot. All this course wants is people who can ride."

" I like that ! " said my cousin Cecilia, who was next. " Just you watch me." And to my amazement and humiliation she also managed to do a clear round.

We spent the next half-hour watching the Cholly-Sawcutt girls making the whole place look like a bomb site, and by the time we got it straightened out again some of the little ones rode and did very well indeed. The funny thing was that when we had all had a turn, it was the people who were really good who did so badly. We were all inclined to giggle about this, except Val Heath who took her riding frightfully seriously since she had once won a prize at Richmond Horse Show.

" I don't know what's the matter with me," she kept saying, and her sister Jack said, " It's either your legs, or you've put on weight."

" Oh, don't be silly," said Val as her pony gave a half-rear. " I think all these jumps want reorganising, the distances are wrong."

" Well of course if you want the whole place altered specially for you—— " said Clarissa, and Cecilia said— with perfect truth—" I should think if I could do a clear round anybody could."

" Well, let's all have another go," I said, and this time I managed to do a clear round, though I had an awful moment when Rapide neighed as we approached the gate and I thought he was going to run out. This time

Val Heath also managed a clear round, but her sister was all over the place in spite of using her stick a lot more than she ought to have done.

" It isn't all that easy," said Diana, and John Watson said, " Well, you don't want it to be, do you ? I think this is teaching us all a lesson, that we've got to improve our jumping, especially those of us who think we're good because we've won a few cups. I vote that instead of trying to show off and jump clear rounds we ought to concentrate more on jumping *well*—never mind whether we get over or not. For instance, I've just done a clear round but I know I had daylight between me and the saddle at the bar jump " ; and Clarissa said, " You're telling us ! I could see the whole county between your legs."

" John's quite right," I said. " In a riding club, we're not competing with each other, we're working to improve our riding and to help the young ones " ; to which Diana said, " Really, grandmamma ? " and Ann said, " One gets a bit too much of encouraging the young entry."

" Let's give the young ones half an hour now," said John, " or they'll think they're not being encouraged at all."

So we started coaching the young ones, and showing people how not to flap their legs about, and not to use their sticks except at the right time and place, and not to jump on a short tight rein or burst into tears if they got three refusals.

It was very hot and tiring, and I got the worst of it as I had a child who thought she could jump anything and was so awful that she ought to have been on a leading rein.

" Pauline, for goodness sake ! " I said. " Let the pony do it ! You haven't got to drag her up by the reins. And if you do pull her head up like that and suddenly let the reins go, of course you'll fall off. And don't say Hup when you don't mean Hup. Don't say Hup at all, you're not up to that stage yet."

" My pony knows what I mean," said Pauline huffily.

" She must be a marvellous mind-reader," I said, " because I don't think you know yourself. Come along now, and do try to remember what I told you about your legs."

By now we were all worn out except John Watson, who very gallantly stood in the middle and made his pupils go over and over two low jumps while he criticised and gave advice.

" What would you do ? " he complained. " When I shout for them to take off they don't ! "

" Oh, leave it, John," I said. " We've all had enough for today, and the ponies are over-excited. We'd better pack it up."

Nobody really wanted to go home, but we were all tired and we felt we had had a terrific day and achieved quite a lot, so we tidied up the jumps and went home, after arranging to come again next morning.

" Well, I think the Greenlee Riding Club is now well and truly launched," said Ann as we rode wearily but happily home through the evening sunlight. The fields were shining like gold on either side of the lane and little rabbits were popping out to sit contentedly munching their suppers.

" Yes, it's going to be a success," I said, " only we'll have to work like blacks if we're going to put on our own gymkhana."

"Wasn't Major Hooley decent?" she said. "It's a funny thing how people start off by being the most frightful clots and then suddenly become nice when you know them better. Even Miss Durdon; and Clarissa wasn't too bad today."

"It's the noble cause of equitation," I said. "It does bring out the best in people."

I really did feel on top of the world, and went home singing a melancholy song called *The autumn leaves must perish*, as I always do when I feel happy. Mummy said I looked like a tramp, and I certainly was a mass of brushwood and whitewash from head to foot. I rubbed Rapide down and gave him his supper, and then I went and had a long and boiling hot bath during which I sang *The autumn leaves must perish* through about seventeen times, until Mummy banged on the bathroom door and said, Must we have that dreary row ? I said it would be much drearier if I sang something cheerful, as that would mean that I was In The Depths.

I then went down and ate an enormous tea, with rounds and rounds of hot buttered toast, and jam and shrimps and chocolate biscuits.

However my day was not ended, as I had hardly finished my tea when who should appear but Stanley Trimble to ask if he could have a lesson.

He was a very nice boy, though he looked rather shaggy and had to keep pushing his hair back. I couldn't say it wasn't convenient to give him a lesson, as his father had been so decent to me about the gate, so I said I would give him half an hour on Black Boy who is a very good pony with beginners, having suffered all my own early efforts.

As we walked to the orchard Stanley said, " I can stick on anything with four legs."

I said that wasn't really the idea in riding, unless one's only object in life was to be a second Dick Turpin or that dreary man who took the good news from some-where to somewhere else ; and Stanley said, " Oh, but I do want to learn to ride properly."

I went to my tack room and got out a leading rein, and Stanley said suspiciously, " What's that for ? " as if he thought I was going to start by hanging him.

I said, " It's to lead the pony by, until I see how you ride. I don't want you to start by losing control and galloping all over the place."

I saddled Black Boy, and then said, " Can you mount ? " Stanley said, " Of course," and putting both

arms across the saddle he leapt up as if he was climbing
a stone wall.

I said that way might do if he was escaping from Red
Indians, but not otherwise, so I explained how he should
mount.   I put his hand on the pommel and his foot in
the stirrup and said, " Now get up properly."

He really did know the way, only he dropped the
reins and I told him off about that.   Then I made him
get down and do the whole thing three or four times,
after which he managed it alone, quite nicely.   Then
I fixed on the leading rein and walked him round, and
thanked my lucky stars when I found that he had
naturally light hands and didn't haul and pull.

He said, " Do you think you could take that leading
rein off, it makes me feel about six," and as he was
riding quite quietly I did so.   He just went on riding
round and round contentedly, though really it was
Black Boy who was doing it all, and would have gone
on at an extended walk for ever and ever.

" Am I all right ? " he said.   " Can't I canter now ? "

I told him he could try, but needless to say he knew
nothing about how to canter ; he simply dug in his heels
and grabbed Black Boy's mane, and as my pony was not
used to that sort of thing he gave a startled snort and
bucked Stanley off.

He picked himself up and said, " That's the first
animal who ever threw me."

" You surprise me ! " I said sarkily.   " Black Boy
isn't in the habit of throwing anybody.   It's your bad
riding."

He took this remark very well, and said, " I suppose
you know."

I said, " For goodness' sake, don't rein him in like

that, it makes his neck ache. You can control him
perfectly well by letting him walk out, and you've got
an awful fault, Stanley. When in doubt you take your
feet out of the stirrups, I never saw such a thing."

He said, " Well, cowboys do it in films," and I said,
if all he wanted was to be able to ride like a cowboy he
was wasting my time giving him lessons.

" All right," he said, " I'll keep my feet in, only
sometimes they slip out." I said they couldn't possibly
slip out if he kept his knees up and didn't turn his toes
down, and I told him he had better learn off by heart
my useful little poem :

> " Hands down and head up,
> Heels down and heart up,
> Knees close to your horse's side,
> Elbows close to your own."

Stanley was impressed, and said he would like to
have the poem written out and pin it to the wall over
his bed, and I said that was all right so long as he had
it in his head too.

" I've forgotten how it goes already," he said. " Is
it ' knees down and head up ' ? Or ' hands down '—
oh, blow ! "

I gave a hollow groan and said, " You'd better write
it in letters a foot high. Now this time get it right."
I said it for him again, and then we unsaddled and
went in the house.

Just at that moment Mrs. Trimble arrived, and was
so disappointed that the lesson was over as she had
wanted to see Stanley on the pony, so in my goodness
of heart—which is always letting me down—I went back
and saddled Black Boy again, and Stanley got up and
sat quite decently, and Mrs. Trimble said he looked a

perfect picture, which is hardly what I would have said as he did look distressingly shaggy, and I thought I would have to use some tact and try to get him to have his hair cut.

Stanley said, would he be able to join the riding club now?

What could I say but yes, though I told him I hoped he wouldn't set a bad example to the younger ones, and he thought a bit and then said what all beginners say the minute they find they can sit on a pony, " When can I start jumping ? "

I gave another groan and said, " As soon as I consider you've learnt to ride."

Mrs. Trimble said, " Oh, but Stanley can ride very nicely already. Now say thank you for the lesson, Stanley," and Stanley said, " Thanks very much for the lesson. When can I come and have another one ? "

I was so tired when I tottered up to bed, I couldn't have been more tired if I had ridden to York and back, as most highwaymen seemed to do in the eighteenth century, but it had certainly been a very good day.

CHAPTER VII

Our Very Own Jumps

I HAD a pleasant surprise next morning, when who should turn up at the crack of dawn but Stanley Trimble again, to say that he had come to help me muck out so we'd be in good time for the rally.

"What rally?" I said, wondering if I'd missed something.

He said, "The riding club rally," and I said I hoped he wasn't going to have his young hopes shattered but it wasn't going to be anything quite as well organised as that; and he said perhaps it was what you'd call a Working Rally, and I said that would be near enough.

He said kindly, "You go and get yourself dressed, and I'll finish this." He really was a decent kind of boy.

I had on my old jodhs already, so I whizzed upstairs and put on a clean yellow shirt and my new fawn tie, and when I came down Stanley was already up on Black Boy.

I said, "You're sitting too far back"—because being his teacher I thought I'd better not let him get away with faults.

He came forward but held his reins too long.

"Look," I said, "your reins are too long."

"You told me yesterday," he said, "not to hold them too short."

"Yes," I said, "but don't lose contact with the pony's mouth. You've got to use your common sense."

We set off, and I told Stanley not to push, and to give his aids more gently. He really was doing quite well.

When we got to the paddock we found a lot of people had already arrived, and Clarissa Dandleby, full of strength and joy, with her plaits flopping and her big specs glaring, was prancing about over the jumps in front of an admiring crowd of kids. She bucked just once too often and came off with a mighty thud. She certainly didn't know how to fall.

"Never mind," she said. "It takes seven falls to make a horsewoman."

It was my private opinion that some people could have seventy and not be any nearer, but I didn't say anything, and I picked all the bits of brush and grass off Clarissa and gave her back her enormous specs which had landed at my feet.

"I thought we'd better give these kids some hot schooling," she said, "and then have a jumping competition for ourselves, just to put a bit of kick in the proceedings."

"Kick will be the word, if you don't catch your pony," said Ann, and Clarissa went loping off after Havelock, who was trailing his reins and cantering happily round and round the other ponies.

She caught him and came back, and announced, "A book I have says that all the best riders fall off."

"Possibly," said Diana Bush drily, "but falling off doesn't mean that you're one of the best riders."

The last thing I wanted was a full-scale argument with Clarissa, so when I saw her taking breath and opening her mouth to retort, I said quickly, "At the risk of being unpopular, what do you say if we teach

these kids something useful, like reining back or turning
on the forehand ? "

"They'll think that's awfully dull," said Diana, and
I said, "Well, they don't come here just to enjoy
themselves."

"Good gracious ! " said my cousin Cecilia. "Surely
everybody can rein back and turn on the forehand ? "

"You'd be surprised," I said. "Anyway, would
you like to get them round you and demonstrate ? "

Cecilia went red, and said, "Oh, I don't pretend to
be a riding teacher. It's possible to do a thing well
one's self and not be able to show other people how."

I had an answer for this, but didn't use it, as I had to
be rather careful with Cecilia. After all she was my
elder cousin, and was sixteen and had left school.

In the end, the reining-back lesson fell to me, assisted
by Ann ; and we had a very warm time with the
younger ones. Some of them weren't bad at all, but
practising reining back isn't a thing you can do too
much of, for the sake of the ponies who don't enjoy
being backed into by inefficients.

June Cholly-Sawcutt announced, "Father thinks
you're doing me a lot of good."

I couldn't help thinking bitterly that Captain Cholly-
Sawcutt with all his experience might have tried to do
his own daughters a bit of good himself instead of
leaving it to a person like me.

However I had my reward when April announced,
"Father says that we can have a rally at our place one
day, and he'll inspect us."

"Did he really say that ? " I gasped.

"Yes, he did," said April. "He's awfully interested
in the riding club."

This was such good news to me that I whooped, and Clarissa who was still showing off by doing half-passes in front of several younger people, said, " What's the excitement ? "

" Oh, nothing," I said airily. " Nothing at all— except that Captain Cholly-Sawcutt is going to invite us to his place for a rally."

" Just a selected few of us, I suppose," said Clarissa.

" No," I said firmly. " The whole shoot, or none at all. This is a riding club, not a private do for people who think they're good."

Cecilia who was hovering near, said, " Well, I never ! I don't have to look far in front of me for somebody who thinks she's good ! "

" Look," I said. " There are just two things I want to say. One is that it's jolly bad form for us big ones to argue in front of the little ones ; and the other is, Clarissa, that if you want to do half passes, do them as a lesson and show the others how they're done."

" Hear, hear," said Ann. " This is no place for showing off."

Clarissa said she was perfectly willing to show anybody how to do half passes, so we picked out a selection of pupils for her and left her to it.

Remembering last time and how bad the riding round had been, I collected a number of people and suggested that we should do a bit of walking and halting. As I feared, this made me very unpopular.

" More baby stuff ! " said David Neville.

" You can't say it isn't needed," I said. " Last time we rode round the ring both the walking and the halting were appalling."

He said that people could practise that at home, and

I said, Yes, but they didn't, and what was the use of practising if they didn't know how to practise?

"All right," he said generously, "I'll help." And he stopped the grumblers for me and got about ten people walking round.

"These are all pretty bad," he said. "Go on, Jill, tell them what's wrong with them."

"For one thing, they're not walking out," I said. "They're just meandering. People aren't using their legs."

"Yes, I am using my legs," said a girl called Hilda Marshall, scowling at me. "One thing I do know is how to use my legs."

"Well, use them differently," said John Watson, coming to my rescue. "Your pony's taking short, quick steps. If you'll loosen your reins a bit she'll take longer, slower ones."

"If I loosen my reins I'll lose control," said Hilda.

"No, you won't. You've got much too short a rein anyway. Your pony can't get her neck out, so she can't take a longer stride."

"If I give her a long rein she'll bolt," said Hilda gloomily.

"Don't be silly. If she tries to bolt, pull her up to a walk and start all over again. That's elementary."

"Oh, can't we canter and jump?" said one or two who were walking correctly and getting tired of it.

"No, you can't," said John. "You can't possibly jump properly until you've mastered simple schooling, and if you don't jump properly you'll never win at gymkhanas. When _I_ consider you've finished schooling at the walk you can begin schooling at the canter, and not before."

F

One or two said that they had already won jumping competitions, and John said that was probably more by good luck than good riding. Just when I felt the whole thing was getting out of hand, who should appear but Major Hooley, and for once I was quite glad to see him.

He stood and watched us for a bit without speaking, and everybody tried to do as they'd been told.

" That's much better," he said. " Now prepare to halt. Halt ! "

The halt was very bad indeed, and I felt that Major Hooley would have been justified in saying something scathing, but he showed remarkable patience and merely said, " Will somebody kindly tell me what you are supposed to do when told to prepare to halt ? "

Everybody looked blank and there was a deathly hush. This went on so long that I had to say something, and I said, " Tighten your fingers and close your legs ? "

" That's quite right," said Major Hooley. " Why put it in the form of a question when you know it's right ? Then, what ? "

" Well, I put my shoulders back and feel the reins until the horse begins to halt," said John.

" Right again," said Major Hooley. " Now all you've got to do is to get those simple instructions rammed into the heads of other people, and then put them into practice. Go to it."

John and I went to it until we were very hot. By then the halting had improved a bit. Major Hooley suggested that we should do a bit about correcting legs and hands, and we had a round or two without stirrups.

" It's no good me doing everything right if the pony

won't do anything right," complained Ann's young sister Pam. " He only obeys me when he feels like it."

" We'll have to have some lessons on improving ponies," I said, " but at the moment I feel too hot, and anyway the ponies must be fed up."

" Yes, we'll call the instruction off for now," said Major Hooley kindly. " I must say, you seem to have a more co-operative lot of people than the first time I came."

" They've been weeded out," I said. " Some of the no-goods didn't come again after the first rally, and we're better off without them. This lot are reasonably keen."

" You and young Watson here seem to be doing all the hard work," said Major Hooley. " What are those other people doing at the jumps ? Amusing themselves ? "

" I think they're doing a competition," I mumbled.

" Let's go over and have a look."

The jumping competition seemed to be between Val and Jack Heath, Diana, Clarissa, Cecilia, and David Neville. A lot of people were standing round watching, including Mercy Dulbottle who said sadly, " I can't jump and I don't suppose I ever shall."

" You won't if you don't try," I said.

" I wouldn't dare, except after dark," said Mercy. " Aren't these people marvellous ? "

" They've all won lots of jumping competitions," I said, " but do get it out of your head, Mercy, that other people are marvellous. Nobody's marvellous in riding. Anybody can make the most frightful mistakes."

" I wish I could practise a bit by myself," said Mercy, dolefully, " when nobody else was here."

"If you'll come round to the cottage some evening I might help you," I said, being noble again without intending to. "Now what have we got here?"

What we had got was Val Heath, preparing to jump a round.

"We've made all the jumps higher," she said. "It's too silly doing two-foot-six and three-foot jumps when we practically never do anything but four-foot ones at home."

"All right, go on," said Major Hooley without commenting.

Val cantered a circle and then jumped a clear round. It was a very neat and pretty performance.

Major Hooley said, "Next one, please."

The next one was Diana, who looked at me as much as to say that this jump-raising wasn't her idea at all. Her pony was good but she managed him badly, and he showed his resentment by a first refusal at nearly every jump. At the second time of asking he went over nicely, but obviously by his own skill and not by reason of Diana's aids.

"That's not jumping," said Major Hooley. "That's sitting on a pony while he jumps."

"I know," said Diana frankly. "The jumps were too high and I oughtn't even to have tried them."

"It's a pity the fences are so narrow," said Clarissa preparing for her own round. "Havelock is used to hunting and he likes his fences wide, or at least with good wings, not these silly little makeshifts."

Round she went, and Havelock tipped pretty well everything with his forelegs.

"There," said Clarissa. "See what I mean?"

"Only too well," said John Watson meaningly.

Clarissa flared up and said that Havelock jumped five foot jumps regularly, only these were enough to put any good pony off.

" Well, if they're so narrow and so awful, isn't it a pity you made them so high ? " said John.

Nobody did well over the raised jumps. Cecilia's horse knocked the stile for six, brought down the brush fence and ran out. The Neville boy did a fairly good round but his style was awful.

" There you have it," said Major Hooley. " If you'd been content to jump the lower jumps to perfection you'd all have looked less foolish. As it was, you had to press, and as a result your timing was lost, or you pushed hard, or your legs weren't ready, or your ponies were either in front of the bit or behind it. And as a demonstration of jumping, I don't think this was a very good example to the less experienced riders, do you ? "

" No, it wasn't," said Val Heath. " It was a bad show. And I'm all for putting the jumps down again."

Nobody could say anything to this, as Val was easily the best jumper of any and had done the only decent round. Clarissa began to natter on about her hunter being too good for narrow fences and anything less than five-foot jumps, but to my surprise my cousin Cecilia suddenly showed traces of sanity by remarking, " I think it would have been better if we hadn't put the jumps up. I'd much rather do a three-foot jump well than a four-foot one badly. After all, style is what counts."

This, of course, started an argument with the Neville boy, on the lines of " Pooh, style ! Just like a girl.

Good riding is all that counts," and Cecilia saying,
" Well, good riding is style, so don't try and be
tough."

Major Hooley then suggested that we should give
the younger ones a chance on a few low jumps without
stirrups, to make them use their legs properly ; so
though we were nearly staggering with exhaustion and
heat by now we nobly did this.

Then he went away, and Ann said, " What a slave-
driver ! "

" I think it's a jolly good thing," I said, " that we've
got a grown-up to take an interest and give a few orders.
I couldn't have coped without him, and Clarissa would
have taken charge, and it would have been a muddle.
I think it's decent of the old boy."

We then declared the rally over, and everybody
began to go home. I hoped the Cholly-Sawcutt girls
would remember to remind their illustrious father that
he had promised us a rally.

Ann and I rode our tired ponies home, and stopped
on the way at a lemonade stall where we each had about
a gallon, which set us back three shillings.

While we were drinking this highly-coloured but
cooling brew who should come along but Mercy
Dulbottle.

" Oh, Jill," she said, " do you think I could come
home with you now and have a jumping lesson, like you
promised ? Aunt Henrietta has gone to town and its
so boring to go home by myself."

The last thing that appealed to me was the idea of
putting Mercy over a bar on the ground and giving her
a few elementary ideas of timing, but seeing she had
got us the field I couldn't very well say no, especially

as I had been the one to tell Ann she had got to be decent to Mercy. So I said, "Okay, you can come along if you like."

We went to the cottage. Mummy was out, but had left a stack of sandwiches. Mercy and I hurled ourselves on this repast. Then while Black Boy and Rapide stood idly watching us, swishing their tails under the cool orchard trees, I dragged myself and Mercy into the hot sun and put a bar down on two bricks, about six inches high.

"See what you can do with that," I said.

Mercy said, "I'm nervous."

"Help!" I said.

Looking like a grasshopper with rheumatism, Mercy walked her pony over the bar and said, "How's that?"

"Jump him," I said. "Don't walk him."

"I don't know how."

"Perhaps he does," I said sarkily. "Give him a chance."

Mercy brought her pony round to the jump again, and this time it seemed to occur to his dim brain that it *was* a jump he was facing. He got terribly excited, his head went up and his quarters went sideways.

"Oh, oh, oh, oh, oh!" yelled Mercy. "Oh, help!"

The pony rushed at the small jump as though it were a hurdle and leapt over it with at least a foot to spare. Then away he loped round the field and Mercy clung on with everything she'd got. She made no attempt to pull him up, and at last he quietened down and brought her back to me at a smug trot. I was quite glad to see her all in one piece, as I didn't want to be the cause of her death.

"I jumped it!" she said, panting.   "Jill, I jumped
it!"

"You're quite hopeless," I said.

She looked dashed, and said, "I don't see why you
should say that.   I want to get good enough to ride in
competitions."

I said, "Well, they say that anybody can do anything."

"But I really did jump it," said Mercy.   "When I
felt myself flying over I nearly passed out."

"So did I," I said grimly.   "If you want to have
another try you can, and this time you'll make an effort
to do it properly."

"What, jump it all over again?" said Mercy, as though she had just done a steeplechase course.

"Don't be silly," I said. "The jump is so low that you should hardly notice it. In fact I'm going to make it a bit higher." I raised the bar by a couple of extra bricks. "Now! Keep calm, don't press, and leave it to the pony."

"But that's what I did before, and he jumped a mile into the air and then simply flew round the field."

"That was because you had no control over him. Not one scrap. Grip him with your knees, and keep your balance, and go *with* him. Let him feel he's being ridden, but for goodness sake don't hang on to the reins to keep your balance or you'll jag his mouth and then he'll refuse to jump at all. Keep your legs firm, and lean slightly forward."

"Oh, what an awful lot to remember," Mercy moaned.

"You've got to go on until you don't have to remember it, it becomes second nature."

"I'll try," said Mercy. "When do I say Hup?"

You don't say it at all," I said patiently. "Not for a one-foot bar."

Mercy got over, and not too badly. She was the most earnest person I had ever taught. She was so earnest that she reduced me to a shred, and she did that little jump again and again, and was so pleased with herself it might have been a five-foot hurdle.

I told her to go home and make herself a low jump, and practise over it without stirrups and her arms folded. She looked at me as if I'd suggested she should stand on her head in the saddle.

I was afraid I was going to have her on my hands for the rest of the night, but at last Mummy came home and called me in. I disentangled myself from Mercy's thanks, and mopped my streaming brow.

CHAPTER VIII

A Pony For Stanley

STANLEY TRIMBLE was beginning to jump quite nicely. He seemed to have a natural talent for it, and a week later Mr. Trimble asked me if I would like to go with them to buy a pony for Stanley.

I was very pleased at this idea, because next best to buying a pony for myself there is nothing I would rather do than buy a pony for somebody else.

We got the local *Exchange and Mart* and spread it out on the Trimbles' kitchen table, while Mrs. Trimble took a tray of hot jam tarts out of the oven and passed them round.

"You know a lot more about this sort of thing than I do," said Mr. Trimble to me, which was flattering but probably incorrect.

We all leaned over the table and breathed heavily on the paper.

"Here it is," said Stanley. "Horses, etc. for sale. What does etc. mean? Giraffes, and things? I'd rather have a horse than an etc."

"This one sounds all right," said Mr. Trimble, pointing. "Bay pony, show jumper, 14.2, three years, spirited, one owner, sure winner."

"Too good to be true," I said briskly. "What about this . . . 'grey pony, 14.2, suitable ride for child.'"

"Oh gosh!" said Stanley in disgust. "I don't

want a suitable ride for a child. I'd rather have
' chestnut mare, 15 hands, very sound, useful hack, has
hunted.' "

" I'm never very taken with ' has hunted,' " I said.
" It usually means the animal is over twenty years old.
And you can't ride anything over 14.2, Stanley. I
know what I'm talking about."

" Yes, Jill knows what she's talking about," said Mr.
Trimble valiantly. " You leave it to Jill, Stanley.
She knows all about buying ponies."

This made me feel a bit cold with responsibility, and
reminded me of the occasion which you may remember
reading about in one of my previous books, when I
had gone out to buy myself a show jumper and returned
with a fifteen-year-old hack, because I liked the look
of her, and a poor wretched little pony that a man in
a cart had been knocking about.

" I still like the ' suitable for a child,' " I said, " and
that doesn't mean it's a kid's pony, Stanley. It probably means it's suitable for show-riding for anybody
in the under-sixteen classes. Do you think we might
go and see it, Mr. Trimble ? "

We wrote down the address, and in the afternoon we
set off in the Trimbles' car ; and Stanley was very
excited as if the pony was as good as bought, while I
had my doubts, which made me feel I must be getting
old, aged people being noted for their lack of enthusiasm
even about horses.

When we got to the house Stanley cried, " That must
be him ! " and we saw a grey pony in a small paddock.
I felt slightly gloomy, because I realised that in one
particular at least the advertisement had lied. The
pony was certainly not 14.2, and I thought 12.2 was

nearer the mark, which would be no use to Stanley.
We knocked at the door, which was opened by a woman
in a red beret, a cotton frock, a diamond brooch and
Wellingtons.

She said, " Oh, have you come about the pony ?
It'll break my little boy's heart to let him go."

I thought, Well why sell him, then ?

I said, " Could we see him, please ? "

She said, " Is that the little boy he's intended for ? "
and Stanley went absolutely scarlet with rage at being
called a little boy, and I could see that so far as he was
concerned the deal was off already.

We went along to the paddock, and the woman—
whose name was Mrs. Webster—said, " Well, there he
is. He'd do with a good clean up, but he only gets dirty
again, so why bother ? "

This peculiar reason for not grooming ponies struck
me with such force that I could only gasp. Meanwhile
Mr. Trimble was looking the pony over and said, " He's
got a sensible head and nice clean legs, but isn't he a
bit under-sized ? "

" You said in the advertisement, 14.2," I said to
Mrs. Webster, " but he only looks about 12.2 to me."

She looked very apologetic, and said, " Well, perhaps
he is. I didn't really know, so I just guessed."

I felt as if every remark of Mrs. Webster's was taking
my breath still further and further away ; and it really
was the climax when Mr. Trimble asked why she was
selling the pony if her little boy would be so upset
about it, and she replied that he had got tired of riding
and wanted a super-speed sports bike instead of the
pony, and though he really would break his heart
when the pony went away he would be consoled by the

fact that the money he got for the pony would pay for the super-speed bike. I thought he must be a soul-less child.

Stanley said, " I think he's too small for me, don't you, Jill ? " and I said, " Oh yes, he wouldn't be any good for you, Stanley."

Mrs. Webster looked awfully depressed, and said the pony was very cheap, only fourteen pounds, and perhaps we knew of some other child who was wanting to buy one.

I said, I supposed he was schooled for the show ring, and could he jump ? And she said, she didn't understand much about schooling, and he could jump a *bit*, and her child had ridden him in several gymkhanas but had never won anything, and they had always kept him more as a pet.

Mr. Trimble said, " He's a nice pony," and I said, yes, but apparently unschooled and therefore dear at fourteen pounds. Mrs. Webster looked as if she was going to cry, and said perhaps she might take twelve, though that wouldn't go far towards the super-speed sports bike.

Mr. Trimble looked so sympathetic that for one awful moment I thought he was going to buy the pony just to stop Mrs. Webster from crying, but I managed to catch his eye in time and said, " It's a pity the pony isn't going to be any use to us, but thank you for showing him to us, Mrs. Webster."

Mr. Trimble looked relieved, and five minutes later we were out of the gate.

" Fancy anybody wanting a bike instead of a pony," said Stanley, and I said, " He must be pretty revolting."

Stanley said, " What do we do now ? It looks as if

I wasn't going to get a pony," and I said, "Oh, don't
be so hopeless," and Mr. Trimble said, "What about
slipping over to Ryechester? It's market day and
they always have some horses for sale."

I said, if there was one thing upset me it was going
to a horse sale because I always wanted to buy them
all, and lay awake for hours at night wondering what
soul-less people had bought the ones I'd fancied ; and
Mr. Trimble said, why should the people who'd bought
the horses be any more soul-less than me?

I said, "You've got something there, Mr. Trimble,
but it doesn't alter my feelings," and then he horrified
me by saying that horses were only live-stock after all,
which made me wish I hadn't come, or hadn't had
anything to do with the Trimbles. I don't think he
was really as bad as this sordid remark would lead one
to think.

"Well, what about Ryechester?" he said.

I had a bright idea.

"Couldn't we go round and see Mrs. Darcy?" I said.
"She might know of a pony."

So we went round to the riding school, and Mrs.
Darcy said at once, "There's a lovely pony for sale at
Fortune Farm, if it hasn't gone already. Shall I give
them a ring?"

"What's it like?" said Stanley. "Actually I want
a grey."

"It's a chestnut," said Mrs. Darcy. "Very quiet."

"Oh dash!" said Stanley. "I want a grey, and
I don't want a quiet pony."

"You'll have what you're given," said Mr. Trimble,
which I thought was quite a constructive remark
though a bit hard on Stanley.

Mrs. Darcy rang up Fortune Farm, and came back and said, " If you go round now they'll show it to you."

Mr. Trimble hummed and hawed a bit, and then said that the one thing he couldn't do was go round to Fortune Farm, as he and Mr. Bedwell who farmed Fortune Farm hadn't been on speaking terms for years, owing to some hoo-ha about the drainage scheme.

I said, " Shall I and Stanley go ? " and Mr. Trimble hummed and hawed some more, and said he'd rather have a look at Ryechester Market first, and if all else failed there was always the Fortune Farm pony to fall back on. I thought this was a dim way of going on, but Stanley said, " Whoops ! Perhaps I'll get a grey after all."

So we got back into the car and drove to Ryechester, to the squalid, tram-shed place where they sell the horses.

I knew under my skin that this wasn't a good idea and that something would happen to me, and sure enough there was a dream of a bay mare, 15 hands, and the minute I saw her I forgot everything else in the world except how much I wanted her. Her hogged mane and tail were black, and she had lovely clean legs, a long flexible neck, high withers, and large soft sensible eyes. She looked at me and I patted her neck.

A little bow-legged man who was standing by said, " Now that's a nice job for you, lady. Lovely bit of horse-flesh. I've seen her jump and she's a treat."

" I know," I said miserably. " I can't buy her, I haven't any money, and I've got two ponies already, and I wish I hadn't come."

Mr. Trimble came up and said. " That's not much use for Stanley."

" She'd be of use to anybody," I said wretchedly,
" but of course she's outside the pony class. I knew
it would be like this. I wish we'd gone to Fortune
Farm."

" Come on," he said, " let's look at the ponies. There
are one or two up here."

I tore myself away from the mare and didn't even
look back at her. We went over and inspected the
ponies, but I didn't have my mind on the job at all ;
I was planning some way I could save some rich old
man's life and be given a hundred pounds reward, and
buy the mare, but things like that only happen in
books.

" I like this one," said Stanley, pointing to a wicked-
looking animal with mean eyes and a long back.

" Don't be silly," I said crossly. " You ought to know
a bad pony from a good one at a glance."

" But he looks spirited."

" He'd murder you," I said.

The only other possibility was a rather nice little
roan, at least he was described in the catalogue as roan
but he was quite pinkish.

" Do you think he's a bit thick-set ? " asked Mr.
Trimble.

" No," I said. " He's only over-fed. Perhaps they'd
let me try him round the yard before the sale starts."

A horsy man came up, and as he knew Mr. Trimble
he said I might try the roan pony. He went quite nicely
and had been schooled, but I had the instinctive feeling
that he wasn't going to make a jumper. I didn't want
Stanley to be disappointed.

The horsy man said, " They'll sell him privately if
you'd like to do a deal now."

G

Mr. Trimble asked how much, and the horsy man said the owner was asking eighteen pounds.

" Too much," said Mr. Trimble. " Fourteen's my price."

" They'll get more than that in the sale."

" I'm not giving more than fourteen."

" I don't think I want it," said Stanley. " I want a grey."

" We'll stay for the sale," said Mr. Trimble, " and if we can get this one for fourteen pounds, this is the one we're having, and I don't want to hear any more about a grey."

Stanley sulked, and I wished we weren't going to stay for the sale as I couldn't bear the thought of seeing that mare sold.

However I was doomed to suffer. The mare went for sixty pounds, and my only comfort was that the woman who bought her didn't actually look unscrupulous and hard-hearted, but rather a decent person.

The roan pony fetched seventeen pounds, so we didn't get it, and the black wicked one went for eleven-ten, and Stanley burst into tears, and Mr. Trimble told him not to be a stupid little cry-baby, and I didn't know which I hated most, Mr. Trimble or Stanley.

However we still hadn't bought a pony, and I was feeling very low ; but Mr. Trimble then showed a spark of humanity by suggesting that we went to a café, and after two chocolate ice-cream sodas Stanley and I both brightened up.

" We'll end up at Fortune Farm after all," I said.

Stanley said indignantly, " But I don't want a quiet pony. It sounds beastly and only fit for pulling bath chairs."

"Don't be silly," I said. "Quiet doesn't mean what you think it means. It doesn't mean the pony's a slug, it means it's amenable to schooling."

I was so pleased with this phrase "amenable to schooling" which of course I had got out of a book that I began to smile in a smug, superior way, and Stanley looked impressed.

"Mrs. Darcy wouldn't recommend it if it wasn't a really good pony," I said.

"Fourteen pounds is my price," said Mr. Trimble.

I had a feeling we were going to finish up without any pony at all.

When we got to Fortune Farm we saw the pony in a field being ridden round by a girl whose legs were too long for it.

"Oh it's sold!" said Stanley. "She's bought it."

"More likely she's the owner and has grown out of it," I said.

"You go and ask, Jill," said Mr. Trimble. "I don't like the Bedwells."

So I went up to the girl on the pony and said, "Is this the pony that Mrs. Darcy said was for sale?"

"Yes," she said. "Do you want to buy him?"

"Not for myself," I said. "For this boy."

She said, "Would he like to try him?"

I said I'd try the pony myself, so I rode him round a bit and he was quite a nice ride, and had been well schooled.

I asked if he could jump, and the girl said she had won prizes with him when she was smaller. She put up a bar for me at two-foot six and I jumped the pony over. For myself I thought he was a bit stodgy, but quite a useful animal for Stanley Trimble to start on.

I asked if he had a vet's certificate, and she said there
was one in the house dated the previous week, and she'd
get it for me to see.   I asked how much she wanted for
him, and she said thirteen pounds, so I said, " Just a
minute," and went back and consulted Mr. Trimble
who was slinking in the hedge, out of sight.

Mr. Trimble said, " He sounds okay.   Buy him, and
let's put an end to this nonsense."

I went back to the field and found Stanley already
riding the pony round.

" Do you like him ? " I said, and Stanley said he
wasn't too bad, though he had wanted a grey.   I
cheered him up by saying that he could use this pony
until he had improved himself and then get a grey, and
so the deal was done.   I got the thirteen pounds from
Mr. Trimble and paid for the pony, and the girl gave
us a halter made of dirty knotted rope, and came with
us to the lane.

" Well, that's that," said Mr. Trimble, and was I
thankful !

" I'll have the odd pound, Father," said Stanley.
" Towards some new tack."

The girl, who must have thought Mr. Trimble
slightly mad to be slinking in the hedge all the time, said,
" The pony's name is Stardust."

Stanley said, " I don't like that name.   I'm going to
call him Peter."

I said that ponies didn't like to have their names
altered, but the girl said that Stardust had never
answered to Stardust anyway, so it didn't matter and
he might as well be Peter.

CHAPTER IX

An Invitation

WHEN I got home, April Cholly-Sawcutt was there having tea with Mummy. She looked rather important, and said she had brought an invitation from her father to the riding club to have a rally at their place the following Friday.

We had just a week to get ready. I could hardly wait to get April out of the cottage before I started ringing everybody up to call a practice for the next day. Everybody was rather awed at the prospect of going to Captain Cholly-Sawcutt's place. Miss Durdon herself came along with Mercy, and announced that as President of the riding club she would be going to the rally too. Several of us looked rather stunned at this, as we were not aware that Miss Durdon was President of the riding club ; or anybody else for that matter, as we had never really considered who we wanted as President, but we couldn't say a thing. Even Clarissa Dandleby was dumb, which was the eighth wonder of the world.

Before you could say space-gun Miss Durdon then began acting as President of the riding club. We found ourselves lined up while she drilled us with crisp orders. After a bit, Clarissa couldn't stand it any longer. She went red in the face and mumbled, " We don't do it like that."

" Were you speaking ? " said Miss Durdon. " If so,

speak up. You won't find any mumbling in the show-ring."

Clarissa said, " I only said, we don't do it like that."

" You'll do it as I tell you," said Miss Durdon. " Don't be a silly little girl." Clarissa was so taken back that she nearly fell on her pony's neck and we all started giggling.

In one sense it was a bit useless, as Miss Durdon's schooling belonged to about the period of the Indian Mutiny when you sat well back, nearly on your pony's rump, stuck your legs out in a cavalry-boot kind of way, and held your hands under your chin ; but on the other hand she had lots of authority, and she had everybody in such a state of awe that they obeyed her without a wriggle. Nobody whispered, nobody got out of line, even the ponies seemed to know they had met their match.

" Well that's very creditable," said Miss Durdon at last. " Very creditable indeed. But to see the way you children sit nowadays, my dear father would have swooned. However I suppose there are fashions in riding. If you all obey me as nicely when we get to Captain Cholly-Sawcutt's we shan't disgrace ourselves."

" Help ! " said Ann to me in dismay. " She doesn't mean she's going to give the orders ? "

That was just what Miss Durdon did mean, only fortunately for us when Friday came she had a bad cold and couldn't turn out at all. She sent us a lot of instructions by Mercy, none of which we bothered about.

I knew all the people who hadn't been to the Fairbridge training stables would gasp when they saw that wonderful place. It was a horsy person's dream of bliss. Long rows of loose boxes, perfect horses, a big gravelled yard, green paddocks, and a marvellous jumping field set out with the sort of jumps you find at a first-class Show.

There were twenty-six of us, and when I had got everybody lined up for inspection we didn't look bad at all ; nor did the lining up take so long as I feared, as the more experienced people helped to shove the others into position and hoped this wasn't being noticed. Fortunately it was a very hot afternoon and the ponies didn't feel like being nappy. I ran an anxious eye along the line. Everybody looked amazingly clean and tidy. Everybody's boots were polished, everybody's tie was straight, and only three people hadn't bothered to iron their shirts. These, strange as it may seem, were April, May and June Cholly-Sawcutt.

" Right," I said. " Just freeze yourselves for about five minutes while we're bring inspected."

Captain Cholly-Sawcutt came out of the house with quite a party of friends. He laughed, and said, " Let me introduce the Greenlee Riding Club," and one of the men said, " A very nice turn-out too," the effect of which was rather spoiled when Ann's young sister Pam for some reason leaned over to scratch her ankle, lost her balance, and swung on her pony's neck. This upset two other people who backed raggedly out of line.

" Never mind," said Captain Cholly-Sawcutt kindly. "It happens in the best circles."

The other man asked, " Which are your girls, Fred ? " and Captain Cholly-Sawcutt said quite casually, " The ones in dirty shirts. Need you ask ? " I thought it was a wonderful way to pass it off, rather than die of humiliation.

Captain Cholly-Sawcutt then ordered the whole line
to walk forward, which we did quite successfully ; and
then to rein back, which we also did fairly successfully
as we had been practising hard. We then walked a
circle, trotted and cantered. I tried to avert my eyes
from Mercy Dulbottle who with a smile from ear to ear
was proceeding round at her only pace, a cross between
a lollop and a hop. However at least nine people were
riding so beautifully that I hoped Captain Cholly-
Sawcutt's fascinated eyes would not leave them to rest
upon more sordid sights. In front of me, Stanley
Trimble on the new pony, Peter, was sitting up straight
as I had taught him, though he looked as if he had
pokers pushed down his back and legs. I muttered,
" Knees up ! " with a vicious hiss, and he brought them
up so quickly he nearly hit his chin.

Captain Cholly-Sawcutt said, " Halt. Line up
again."

I had cunningly made arrangements for this to
happen, every good person being responsible for a
duddish kind of person. As soon as the order was given
the good ones collared their " duds " and fairly rammed
them into line, so the whole operation only took about
two minutes, except that my dud was Mercy, and she
kept saying, " What are you *doing*, Jill ? " in a sort of
anguished squeak. I could have murdered her.

" Just a few questions," said Captain Cholly-Sawcutt.
" First one who knows the answer shout it out. What's
the first thing you do when you bring your pony out
of the stable for schooling ? "

Before the rest of us had time to think, Clarissa said
smugly, " I ride him round and let him relax and loosen
up before I begin schooling."

" Quite right. Next question. You wish to give your pony an order, what do you do ? "

" Prepare him, and then apply the aids gently," said Clarissa, all in one breath before anybody else had time to open their mouth.

Captain Cholly-Sawcutt looked a bit dazed, but said, " Correct. You—the boy third from the left—you are sitting slightly too far back. Where is the proper place to sit ? "

David gave a sort of stutter, and Clarissa chipped in, " In the lowest part of the saddle as near as possible to the pommel."

" Er—quite," said Captain Cholly-Sawcutt, looking nervously at Clarissa. " I think that'll do for the questions," he went on, probably afraid that in a minute Clarissa would be asking *him* a few questions that he couldn't answer.

" Show-off ! " muttered Val Heath, glaring at Clarissa, who said, " Well, somebody had to answer and the rest of you were as dumb as coots."

By now we were all rather excited, and I was afraid if the inspection went on much longer there would be chaos among the younger ones. To my relief Captain Cholly-Sawcutt said, " You've done quite well and you're a promising lot. I think we've had enough hard work. You've come here to enjoy yourselves, so just say what you'd like to do. The place is yours for the afternoon."

Of course nobody cared to speak first, and then April Cholly-Sawcutt said the first sensible thing I ever remember her saying. She said, " I think some people would like to do some jumping and some people would like to do some competitions."

This was exactly what we did want.

John Watson said to me, " Do you think he'd let us try his jumps ? "

" They're terribly high," I said. " I'd love to try them if he'd put them down a bit."

" So would I. I'll ask him."

Captain Cholly-Sawcutt said, " Of course. With pleasure," and sent a man to lower the jumps to suit us. They were the most beautiful white-painted jumps, just like a show-ring course, and about half of us had the time of our lives going round them. You know how it is in a jumping competition, you often wish you could have the chance to do one of the jumps again and do it properly. Well, we could do any of these jumps again, and make them higher or lower to suit ourselves. It was the most superb place for practising.

Meanwhile one of the grooms was arranging some competitions for the younger ones, and they had put up the poles for a bending race by the time we had reluctantly decided that our ponies were too tired for any more jumping.

" I wish I had thought to bring a second pony," said Val Heath. " I could have gone on for ever on that lovely course."

" So could I," I said, thinking of Black Boy at home in the orchard.

" Look at those poles," said John Watson. " They're far too close together. No pony could get round them."

" It isn't my fault," said the groom. " I put them the right distance apart but Miss May altered them all."

" I like them close together," said May Cholly-Sawcutt, " because my pony is shaped like a worm and he wiggles in and out."

" Good lord ! " said John.

May then gave an exhibition of how her pony wiggled in and out of the poles which were too close together, and she certainly could do it, but nobody else could have done, so John insisted on putting the poles as they ought to be, and May said, " Now I shan't win the beastly race and it'll be your fault."

John said, " As it's your father's party I suppose you're the hostess and the hostess isn't supposed to win," and May said, " I think that's beastly unfair," which shows what a hopeless sort of person she was.

Mercy Dulbottle said she didn't see why she shouldn't have a try at the bending, it looked easy enough, and Pam Derry said, " It isn't easy at all, you've got to gallop like mad, and if you miss one out you're disqualified and if you knock one down you're disqualified too."

" All right," I said, " if you know so much about it, you go first, Pam."

I picked out another girl about Pam's age and set them off. Pam's pony leapt forward and simply raced down the posts, and was half-way home before the other girl had reached the turn. Pam won by several lengths.

" I could do this standing on my head," she said.

I started off the next two, and when they got back Pam said, " Gosh, don't they dawdle ! It isn't any fun if people don't gallop. Why don't they whack the ponies round ? It's like a slow-motion film."

" If you don't shut up," said Ann to her younger sister, " you can jolly well go home. I'll tell Mummy tonight you're a menace."

Pam piped down a bit, especially as two or three

people did very good races, but when they came to ride off the heats she won again and again, and in the final she again came in by lengths.

"I wish she hadn't won," said Ann. "She's too cocky by miles, and now she'll get the idea she's a star rider."

"She'll soon get it knocked out of her," I said, "if she enters for any open competitions."

"Oh, look at Mercy!" said Ann.

Mercy, who had parted from her pony about a quarter of an hour before while going round the second pole, was still sitting on the ground.

"Are you hurt?" I said.

"I don't know," said Mercy. "I feel as if my backbone's coming through the top of my head."

"Well, it isn't," said Ann. "Do get up, Mercy. You've been told before, you must get up immediately after a fall, or make an effort anyway. Don't be so feeble."

Mercy got on her feet with a lot of "ooh-ing," and said, "Where's my horse?"

"That's for you to say," I said. "You oughtn't to have let the reins go."

"Oh, look, it's over there," said Mercy. "It's lying down. If the horse can lie down I don't see why I shouldn't."

"Oh, leave her alone," said Ann. "She's nuts."

Captain Cholly-Sawcutt then came up and said, how would everybody like to go in for a grand egg-and-spoon race? He would go in for it himself, and also everybody on the premises. We all thought it would be fun.

So everybody turned out and the stable people rode

bareback, and out came Mrs. Cholly-Sawcutt and Pansy and the vet who happened to be there, and all kinds of people, though some of them couldn't ride for nuts and I don't think any of them tried very hard because they obviously wanted members of the riding club to win.

We rode off the heats in fours. Mrs. Cholly-Sawcutt provided four teaspoons and the eggs were knobbly potatoes.

I won my heat, mainly because I was lucky enough to get the least knobbly of the potatoes. Captain Cholly-Sawcutt who was in my heat dropped his potato four times, but he was only fooling about and making people laugh.

Eventually I got into the semi-final but that was the end of me. I dropped my potato, and when I dismounted to pick it up Rapide thought it was part of a game and began to dance about.

By then the heat had already been won by David Neville who was a natural at this kind of thing, and had never once dropped his potato. He easily won the final too, and wasn't even out of breath.

Captain Cholly-Sawcutt gave him a riding stick for a prize, and said he would take it away again if David used it too much or in an improper way.

Then we all went into the big empty barn, and there was a long table spread with lemonade, buns, and cakes, which disappeared like magic.

John Watson said, " I say ! We've got to do a special vote of thanks to Captain Cholly-Sawcutt for all this. I mean, it really is something for a member of the British Show-jumping team to invite a potty little riding club like us to a ' do ' like this."

" Well, you know why he does it," said Ann. " It's for Jill's sake, because she's taken such a lot of trouble with his revolting, unsportsmanlike, and ham-handed daughters."

" Oh I say ! " said John. " April's quite pretty."

" I didn't say she wasn't," said Ann. " I said she couldn't ride."

" About this speech, anyway," began John.

My cousin Cecilia then chipped in, and said, " If there's to be a speech I'm going to do it. I'm the eldest."

" All right," said John. " Nobody particularly wants to do it ; but if you do it, you'd better be good ! "

Cecilia said he needn't worry, she was a whizz at speeches ; and so in fact she proved to be, because not only was she very flowery in her language but she went on for ages until everybody thought she was never going to stop. We were all fidgetting about, and Captain Cholly-Sawcutt who was getting thanked was as red as a beetroot. In the end, Clarissa Dandleby, who was standing next to Cecilia, gave her a kick on the ankle and said gruffly, " Shut up," and strangely enough Cecilia shut up. At least Captain Cholly-Sawcutt couldn't say he hadn't been thanked, as Cecilia had thanked him nineteen times all in different words, I know because I counted.

When it was all over and we got outside, he said to me, " I believe you're running this riding club, aren't you, Jill ? "

I said that I had actually started it, but I couldn't say who was running it. In fact a lot of different people seemed to be doing so.

" What's your aim and object ? " he asked.

" Well, we do want to improve our riding, and we thought it would be a good thing to bring on the younger ones a bit, and let them mix with us in events. It makes things rather friendly. And then we thought we'd run a little gymkhana in about a month's time, and anybody can enter for that, but we hope the riding club members will carry off all the prizes."

He laughed, and said, " I suppose you'll have to beg the prizes from somewhere. You can put me down for three."

" Oh, that is frightfully good of you ! " I said.

" Not a bit. I daresay my wife will give you one. Let me know when you get your schedule ready. In a month, did you say ? That'll be after Chatton Show, I suppose ? "

" Yes, the week after. A lot of us will be riding at the show."

" Any difficulties at the riding club ? " he said. " Anything you need to help you ? "

" I think what we really need," I said, " is a bit of expert instruction for the older ones. We seem to spend a lot of our time teaching the younger ones, but nobody ever teaches us. Except of course Major Hooley, but he gets rather irritated and I don't think he brings out the best in us."

" If you like to call a rally," said Captain Cholly-Sawcutt, " I'll ask a friend of mine to come round and give you an hour. He's very good. Would you like that ? "

" Oh, would we ! " I cried. " I think it's marvellous of you."

So a few days later we met at the field and a Mr. Storm appeared. Miss Durdon wasn't too welcoming to him at first, because she rather resented the idea of any stranger giving us instruction in her field under her very nose, but when they began to talk she found out that Mr. Storm had actually known her father in India, and after that he could do nothing wrong. I kept wishing they would stop talking and get on with the rally. Miss Durdon kept saying, " Did you know old So-and-so ? I always said he'd die with his riding boots on," and Mr. Storm said, " Do you remember Mrs. Thingummy ? She hunted till she was ninety-four."

However, when Mr. Storm did get down to work on us he proved to be very good indeed. Of course, we had to be willing to be told our faults—even in front of the others—but what I say is, if you can't bear to be told where you're wrong you had better sell your pony and buy a sewing-machine or something equally dreary. Mr. Storm was dressed in corduroys and a hacking jacket, and from the minute I saw him handle one or two restless ponies in a nonchalant way, and magically get everybody into perfect order while not seeming to take any trouble at all, I knew he was a flawlessly horsy person.

Miss Durdon kept butting in, with Indian bits about pig-sticking and Yoga.

" I wish the tatty old witch would dry up," said John Watson. " This bird knows what he's talking about, if she'd give him a chance."

" Oh, do be quiet, John," I said. " You've got the most awfully penetrating whisper I ever heard in my life. He'll hear you calling him an old bird, and she'll hear what you say about her, and before we know where we are we shan't have a field or an instructor or even a riding club."

" Don't be silly," said John. " They won't hear,
they're miles away, inspecting the way the ponies are
groomed. By the way, yours could do with a dust
over, couldn't he ? "

I was mad at his superior tone, and pointed out that
the worst of black horses was the way they showed the
dust, and that Black Boy had looked like patent leather
when I left home ; and John said it was the same with
black cars, though he still liked them best.

By now, Mr. Storm was telling everybody to dismount
and take off their saddles. He then went over every
pony in turn, as carefully as a judge in the showing class.
I was thankful for all the grooming I had done that
morning, but one or two people got it in the neck,
including Clarissa.

" How long did you spend in grooming your horse
this morning ? " said Mr. Storm to her.

Clarissa gasped, and said, " None at all. Our groom
sees to all that."

" Well, in this case," said Mr. Storm, " he has seen
to nothing. I don't blame him. If the rider doesn't
care, why should the groom ? However many Arab
steeds I had, each with its own groom, I should still take
off my saddle before I rode out, and inspect my horse's
ears, and see that his hoofs were oiled." Then seeing
that Clarissa's eyes were boiling over behind her specs,
he went on, " On the other hand, I must congratulate
you on your own appearance. You look extremely
neat, and your breeches and boots are spotless, and
your coat well brushed. Your hair is tidy, too, in that
beautiful plait. Not like—" and his eyes swivelled round
to my cousin Cecilia who was wearing her hair in a
long, all-in-one-piece bob that flopped down on her

H

shoulders and made her look like a film extra.   I hadn't
noticed Cecilia's get-up before, or—cousin or no cousin,
elder or not elder—I would certainly have torn her
off a strip for coming to a rally in that sort of
get-up.

" No, no, decidedly wrong," said Mr. Storm, fixing
Cecilia with his glassy eye.   " Push it into your hat,
girl."

Cecilia looked annoyed, and John Watson began to
giggle.

Mr. Storm told Mercy Dulbottle that her girth was
loose enough to go round two horses and stood by while
she fumbled about, tightening it, and Miss Durdon
danced with impatience and said, " Really, Mercy,
really ! " which didn't help things at all.   When it
came to my turn I got off lightly, though he said my
crash cap was a bit to one side and he preferred a plain
tie.   He certainly was frightfully particular.

He then made us ride round a circle, and I could tell
he was concentrating on the people who considered
themselves good riders.   He had some fault to find
with everybody, and I for one was glad of this, because
you do get careless when you think you are good.   He
corrected nearly everybody's seat, and told me that I
was apt to come forward in front of my hands.   Other
people, he said, were too far back, or held the reins too
short, or were not sufficiently relaxed and looked stiff
at the trot.

Then he went on about legs, legs, legs, and here John
Watson got the axe, because I had noticed myself that
instead of keeping his knees close to his pony's sides and
pressing them, he opened them wide and clumped them
in suddenly, which was not only ugly but prevented the

pony from going quietly into a trot or canter. John's movements were jerky, but I must say after he was told he improved a great deal.

"You!" said Mr. Storm to Val Heath, who was probably the best rider of any of us. "You have a perfect pony who understands you so well that she has let you become thoroughly lazy. You are doing no work at all. You are sitting on your pony and thinking how effective you look, because you know she will obey your lightest touch and that all this is child's play. What I want you to do is dismount and change ponies with somebody—anybody, that girl next to you—yes. . . . That's better. Now you have got a pony who is not so good as your own and doesn't know you. Now you will *have* to work, and I shall be able to see if you can really ride."

Val didn't look pleased for a minute, but being a sensible person she soon realised that Mr. Storm was right. She got up on the grey pony, which had a startled eye, a slightly coffin-shaped head, and a barrel body. For a minute she was at a loss, and then she showed she was a real horsewoman by the way she gently but firmly applied the aids and got the pony going at a nice controlled pace, correcting each fault as it occurred.

"Bravo, bravo!" said Mr. Storm. "That is riding. The pony has never been so well ridden before, and he appreciates it. His rightful owner can learn a lesson from this too. It wouldn't be a bad idea if you all changed ponies occasionally."

The girl who owned the pony—her name was the peculiar one of Posy Meadows—looked as happy as a tomtit riding Val's pony, and beamed all over as she

watched Val riding hers and getting such a lot out of
him that Posy hadn't been able to get.

" Dear, dear, dear ! " said Mr. Storm, looking at
Ann Derry. " You have a shocking fault, and you
don't know it, it is just a bad habit you have got into.
You look down to see if your pony is on the right leg.
That is frightful. You know perfectly well when your
pony is on the right leg, and yet your silly little head
has to go down to make sure. You do know, don't
you ? "

" Yes," said Ann. " It's just a crazy habit I've got
into. I must have been doing it for ages without
realising it. I won't do it again."

" I hope you won't, or the next thing that will happen
will be that you'll become the sort of person who looks
back at jumps in the show ring. Nothing can be worse
than that. Do you ever look back at jumps ? "

Ann went red, and said that she couldn't remember,
but she probably did, and Diana Bush nobly said,
" Directly I've done a jump I have the most beastly
feeling that something is sawing my head round to look
back. I have to fight it."

Mr. Storm then picked on David Neville, and said,
" Here you have a case of a rider and a pony who are at
variance with one another. They don't think they are,
but I can see it. All the time there is a struggle going
on ; the pony is trying to escape from the rider's legs
and from his own bit. It is a case of strength against
strength, and that is no good at all. The rider must
be more gentle and relaxed, then the pony will be the
same. What's your name ? "

" David," said David.

" Well, David, I can only tell you, you must feel your

reins and you must keep your legs closed, and you must never, never push. However much you want to push, don't push. You'll find your riding much easier. That's better already. And now, everybody, we're going to trot and canter, change legs smoothly, halt slowly, and rein back. Please concentrate. This has got to be very good."

It was a very strenuous afternoon, but we all had to admit that Mr. Storm had done us a lot of good.

" A few afternoons with him, and I should melt away altogether," said Val Heath. " Gosh, how he made me work on that dud pony of Posy's."

" It's the best thing that ever happened to you," said her sister. " If you can't ride any sort of pony you're not a real rider at all. Next time we have a rally I'm going to borrow a dud from one of the kids and see what I can do with it."

I remembered to go and thank Mr. Storm, who was going back to tea with Miss Durdon to talk about the Taj Mahal and paper-chases in the Punjab, and he said there was no need to thank him, it had been a pleasure to do something for the cause of equitation and he hoped we would all work hard and have jolly good luck in any competitions we entered for, and that he himself would be judging at Chatton Show and would look forward to meeting some of us there. I hadn't realised he was so high up in the horsy world, and I thought we were terrifically fortunate to have had such a man to instruct us, but it just shows that the highest are usually the most humble and willing to help others.

" He was really a decent old lemon," said John Watson as we clattered out into the lane, " though if I do meet him in the show ring I shall feel he has an unfair advantage in knowing which of my faults to look out for."

"Don't worry," said Diana. "He'll have forgotten us all by then ; I hope so, anyway. I think he'll be quite a tough judge, but what's the good of having a riding club unless it makes us improve enough to face tough judges ? I'm all for it."

"Phew, haven't we worked the last few days ?" said Ann. "Couldn't we have some fun next time instead of all this hard labour ?"

So we decided we would have an afternoon of games and races, which would be fun for the ponies as well as for us.

CHAPTER X

Planning A Gymkhana

THE games-and-races afternoon was more of a success for the younger ones than for us experienced ones, as we felt it was our duty to give the young entry a good time and make them think they were getting something out of the riding club. Quite a lot of fond parents came along to watch, and to swoon with rapture at the sight of their tots on ponies shying potatoes at a bucket and missing every time.

A number of people from school came to watch too, and said they had heard we were getting up a gymkhana, and would anybody be allowed to enter or was it just for our members ?

I said, we wanted as many people as possible to enter, whether they belonged to the riding club or not, though of course we hoped that our own members would carry off most of the prizes.

" Isn't it time we did something definite about this gymkhana ? " said John Watson. " When's the thing going to be, anyway ? "

" The Saturday before we go back to school," I said. " That's the first Saturday in September."

" All right. That's one thing arranged. What about judges and schedules and rosettes and prizes and seats for the people who have so little sense as to come and watch us ride ? Gosh, this thing's going to cost money, isn't it ? "

" It won't have to," I said. " We must go round and ask everybody we know to give things."

" My father would be a judge," said Val Heath, " and you needn't be afraid of favouritism, he'll be equally tough with everybody. And I think Mrs. Darcy would be a judge if you asked her, Jill."

" Good show," I said. " That's the judges fixed. What about rosettes ? "

" Easy," said Ann. " If we all put in about three-pence we can buy yards of ribbon at Woolworth's and wheedle our mothers into making them up when they go out to tea with each other. And I'm sure Stanley Trimble's father would provide the ropes for the ring ; and they'd lend us the seats from the Parish Hall for nothing, if somebody would take a lorry to fetch them."

" Stanley Trimble's father ! " yelled about six people in chorus.

" It's all going to be quite simple," said David Neville.

" Not so simple as all that," I said, " because the reputation of the riding club is at stake, and if the gymkhana is a flop we shall feel terribly small and all these weeks of practising will be wasted."

" Oh dear, need we have a gymkhana at all ? " said Mercy Dulbottle, and we all squashed her flat by screaming, " Of course we must have a gymkhana ! What's the good of the riding club if we can't put on a gymkhana ? "

" The most important thing," said Diana Bush, " is the schedule. What sort of events are we going to have ? "

" Perhaps I could have a word here," said Clarissa very loudly. " I vote we draw the line at kiddish events, definitely."

" Don't be silly," I said. " Half the members of the riding club are under fourteen."

" Well, that crowd hardly count at all," said Clarissa. " They're only learners, and they ought to be jolly glad to stand by and watch the rest of us. If you make this gymkhana a kiddish thing nobody worth while will bother to come, and what's more, *I'm* not going to waste my time on it."

" All right, Clever—stop away," said John Watson. " The under-fourteens have got as much right to have their events as we older ones have. Also, considering the help we've had from Captain Cholly-Sawcutt and people like Stanley Trimble's father, and considering that we're going to expect the kids' mothers to work their fingers to the bone making rosettes, the least we can do is to see that *their* kids have a fair chance of competing and winning something."

" Hear, hear ! " I said.

" I'm not thinking so much about the under-four-teens, as the under-tens," said Ann. " If my sister Pam doesn't get a look-in at some event my mother won't be pleased, and I'm counting on her to give us an awful lot of lemonade for the day."

" Right," said John Watson. " Event for the under-tens, in return for a lot of lemonade from Mrs. Derry."

" Of course if you're going on like that," said Clarissa, very snootily, " the whole thing is going to be a farce."

" Oh, go and boil your head," said John. " You old fusspot ! You'll get your senior jumping all right, but Ann's talking sense. We want people who really matter in the riding world to come to our gymkhana and give our riding club a boost, and what will they think if they see the big ones prancing about all the

time and grabbing all the fun ?   They'll think a great
deal more of us if they see we're not being greedy but
giving a fair innings to the young entry."

"Good for you, John," said Val Heath. "Well,
here and now I vote we have a showing class *and* a
game for the under-tens ; they won't take long, because
there won't be many entries.   Also showing and jumping
and a game or competition for the under-fourteens, and
then jumping for us older ones, and an open competition
which the under-fourteens can join in as well.   I think
that gives the juniors a jolly good innings, and really
the best treatment of any section in the club."

"It's ridiculous," said Clarissa, "it only gives us
seniors one event worth calling an event, and that's the
jumping. Surely we can have dressage, or handy
hunter, or something ? "

"It'll be too boring for the spectators," said Diana.
"This gymkhana isn't a pony show, it's supposed to
amuse us and the public.   I'm quite content with the
jumping and an open competition."

"If there's time," said John Watson, "we might have
bareback trotting and cantering for the seniors.   That's
interesting to watch and very good for us too."

"Good idea," I said.   "Have you got some paper,
John ?   Stick it down."

"I vote we make John the gymkhana secretary,"
said Ann.

"Right-oh," I said, and John said, "Well, speaking
with the utmost modesty, I don't think anybody else
would be as good."

He then produced a notebook and a pencil and said,
"Let's stick down what we've got.   We'll start at two,
or one-thirty would be better.   Let's put one-thirty,

showing class, ten and under. Then a game, ten and under. What game?"

"Oh, something frightfully simple, like standing on one leg at the gallop," said Clarissa sarkily.

"If you don't shut up," said John, "you'll be needing an ambulance in about five minutes. The obvious game for the under-tens is Musical Chairs. The parents adore it."

"The ones that don't win," said Clarissa, "will scream, cry, fight, hit their ponies, and run to Mummy."

"Will somebody murder that woman for me?" said John, and to my surprise my cousin Cecilia said, "Oh shut up, Clarissa. Don't be so feeble."

"Next," said John, "we'll have the showing class for fourteen-and-under, followed by—cheers!—tea."

"Tea he says!" I said scathingly. "Where's the tea coming from?"

"Fond parents," said John. "Don't tell me we can't grind some sort of a tea out of people's mothers? They'll want tea themselves, so the least they can do is to provide the cakes and things, and some tea and milk, and we'll have to find somebody who'll lend us a marquee for nothing, and——"

"You don't want much!" said Diana.

"I hadn't even finished," said John with dignity. "They can give the tea, and the marquee, and also make the tea and serve it. They'll love to, if nicely asked. I'll bet my mother will make dozens of cakes and help to serve the tea too. Now where are we up to? I know, junior jumping."

"You've missed out the junior game," I said.

"Oh blow, so I have. What game, do you think?"

"Bending?"

" Potatoes in buckets ? "

" Handkerchiefs on poles ? "

" Hadn't we better ask the juniors what they want ? "
I said. " If we try to wish a game on to them they'll
think they're being swizzled, and make a riot."

" Okay. I'll just put down junior game, and we'll
shove it in before tea. Then some of us hardy types can
spend the tea interval helping to put up the jumps and
get the course ready. After tea, junior and senior
jumping. That'll take ages and we can wind up with
a grand finale, a good competition."

" Gretna Green ! " said Val Heath. " It's terrific
fun to watch and to do, and it brings in all ages. The
seniors can be the bridegrooms and the juniors the
brides. It's good fun."

" Never heard of it," said Clarissa, in a voice which
suggested that all that sort of thing was beneath her.
She then added, trying not to sound curious, " What
do you do ? "

Val explained that the seniors had to mount, race to
a given point where the brides were waiting, dismount,
hoist the bride up behind the saddle, remount, and race
back again. Clarissa said, the main point in that
seemed to be to pick a bride who weighed about two
stone ; and Val said, you didn't pick them, you drew
them out of a hat ; and John Watson said, the under-
fourteens in the riding club were the fattest lot of girls
he'd ever seen in his life, and wasn't there some sort of
race that didn't involve slave labour ?

Clarissa said, " Let's have a hurdle race. You just
go on jumping the hurdles till you knock one over, then
you drop out " ; and I said, " Thank you, I'd rather
not take my pony home buckled up with exhaustion,"

and Clarissa said, What made me think I'd jump all that many hurdles ?

Ann said, " Let's vote on it.   Hands up for the fat brides."

Everybody wanted the Gretna Green race except Clarissa and Cecilia, so it was carried.

" That's O.K.," I said.   " Next thing is to get it all copied out and the schedules printed, John.   The sooner we get the schedules out the better, and then we can start on the entries."

" How much are we charging for each entry ? " asked Diana.

" Well, seeing it's our own riding club we can't charge much," I said.   " I should think threepence each entry for our own members, and sixpence for outsiders.   That ought to make some money to pay for the printing and the ribbon from Woolworths.   And they must pay when they make their entries, to give us some cash to be going on with."

" Shark ! " said Clarissa.

" Shark yourself," I said, which was far from clever, only I was getting too bored with Clarissa to bother to think up any bright retorts.

" That's all, then," said Diana.   " Stick it down, John, and let's see how it looks."

John produced the following schedule.

GREENLEE RIDING CLUB GYMKHANA
at the paddock, Bent Lane.
Saturday, September 9th, at 1.30 sharp.

Class 1.	*Showing Class.*	*Ten and under.*
Class 2.	*Musical Chairs.*	*Ten and under.*
Class 3.	*Showing Class.*	*Fourteen and under.*
Class 4.	*Game.*	*Fourteen and under.*

INTERVAL FOR TEA

Class 5. Jumping. Junior.
Class 6. Jumping. Senior.
Class 7. Gretna Green Race. Open.
Class 8. If time. Exhibition of open bareback
riding, non-competitive.

" I hope it doesn't look too kiddish," said Clarissa.

" You've got kiddish on the brain," said David Neville. " It's probably because you're kiddish yourself that you're so afraid of *looking* kiddish. I think the schedule looks utterly gamoosh."

" Utterly—what ? " I said.

" Gamoosh. Quite the latest word. I'm surprised you haven't heard *that* before," said David.

" I bet he made it up," said Clarissa. " It's the silliest word I ever heard."

" What about numbers ? " said Ann.

" Numbers of what ? " said John.

" Just numbers, you idiot. For the competitors."

" Oh, those. Help ! It just shows what a lot there is to think about. We're sure to forget *something*. Numbers, of course. We can make those ourselves.

" What out of ? "

" Sheets of cardboard, of course, and Indian ink."

" And what's all that going to cost ? "

" Oh, help ! More expense ! " I groaned. " We shall simply have to have some funds."

" Okay," said John calmly. " Uncle John arranges everything, and without fuss. We'll have a White Elephant sale."

" Only we haven't got any white elephants to sell."

" Funny, aren't you ? White elephants are just

things you don't want. You bring them along here,
and somebody else wants them and buys them.
Compris ? "

" Whizzo," said David. " I've a perfectly revolting
tie that my aunt sent me for my birthday. I'll sell it
to anybody for threepence."

" And who do you think would buy your revolting
tie ? Be your age. They've got to be saleable things.
Let's go and tell all the kids to ask their mothers for
things to sell, and tell all their mothers to come to the
sale, and we'll have it here, on the field, tomorrow
afternoon."

I had my doubts about this sale, as those of you who
have read my previous books will remember that once
Ann and I ran a sale and it was by no means a success.
However, this one arranged by John was all right, and
you should have seen what turned up !

There were books and cushions and evening shoes,
and cardigans and blouses, and vases and milk jugs and
photo frames, and dandy brushes that were only a bit
worn, and in fact lots of stable equipment brought by
the Cholly-Sawcutt girls that was so good we practically
fought each other to buy it ; and ties that weren't in
the least revolting, only people's fathers didn't want
them any more, and ash trays, and garden plants, and
tools, and toys.

It was a magnificent sale, only John Watson strutted
about with such an alone-I-did-it smirk on his face that
we all wanted to murder him.

We raised thirteen pounds, which was such a good
start that we all knew we were going to have a smashing
gymkhana, worthy of support by the equitation experts
of the district.

The next thing was to go round asking people to give us prizes, which we felt was a bit thick on top of everything else, but the response was marvellous. We got string gloves, ties of a horsy nature, ties of a less horsy nature, two tie-pins with foxes' heads on them, stable brushes and rubbers, two large tins of saddle soap, six teaspoons in a velvet case, a lovely pair of stirrups—from Captain Cholly-Sawcutt, and I thought whatever else I didn't win I wanted to win those—and a small silver cup which was the *pièce de résistance*, presented by Miss Durdon for the senior jumping class.

"The stirrups had better be the first prize for the junior jumping," said David Neville, who was fourteen.

A lot of us felt a bit dashed at this idea, which put the seniors out of the running. I wasn't the only one who wanted those stirrups, by a long shot. In the end we decided we'd have them for the first prize in the Gretna Green race, which gave both seniors and juniors a chance.

"That's not much good," said Clarissa. "Do the winning pair get one stirrup each?"

"Blow!" said Ann. "It only wanted that."

"I think the only fair thing," said David, "is to make them the first prize for the junior jumping. We ought to give a decent prize for that."

We agreed that that was the fairest thing to do with the stirrups, and all the juniors at once began talking about what they'd do when they won them.

"They'll probably be won by some awful type who isn't even a member of the riding club," said David.

We allocated the rest of the prizes, and then Miss Durdon announced that she would like to give a special riding prize for an event of her own invention.

" It will probably be for the one who has made the most progress," she said, " and the judges will decide. I shall be one myself."

We all felt a bit overcome at this idea, as we already had for judges Mrs. Darcy and Val Heath's father—which for a small gymkhana was quite enough—but after what Miss Durdon had done for us we had to let her be on the panel if she wanted to, and she obviously did.

CHAPTER XI

Across Country

IT was absolutely tropical weather, and when I got home after making all those arrangements I said I was worn to a shred.

Mummy said rather acidly, so was she—from hearing about nothing but horses from morning till night, and did it never occur to me that there were other worthwhile things in the world that I might and could do?

I said I quite agreed that there were other worthwhile things in the world, and for the people who cared about doing those other worthwhile things it was very nice that there were those things to do, but Mummy had said herself that it was better to do one thing properly than a lot of things in a mediocre manner, and therefore she ought to be glad that I was doing properly the thing that I considered most worthwhile instead of wasting time on doing a bit of this and a bit of that.

Mummy said, " Really, Jill, you are the most hopeless person to argue with ; you think you know all the answers, and what about the world of art, to which you haven't a clue ? "

I said I was quite ready and willing to take an interest in the world of art, and Mummy produced a picture of a rather brownish nature which she had bought at a sale, and told me to hang it in my room and look at it often ; which I did, though I must admit it never looked to me like anything but a woman in a dressing-gown leaning on a pile of plates.

By now John Watson had bought the cardboard and Indian ink, and he and one or two others came round

to the cottage in the evening and we worked like mad, making the numbers.

I knew Mummy was dying to mention several ways in which we might be better employed, but she didn't say anything, and after about an hour of toil we looked up to see her appearing with a tray of orangeade, iced buns, and chocolate biscuits, which made me want to hug her there and then.

"Gosh!" said John Watson. "Isn't your mother decent? Mine would probably have made some searing remark about, couldn't four healthy teenagers find something more useful to do on a fine summer evening?"

I didn't say anything, but I thought, it just shows.

The numbers looked marvellous, and not at all smeary, and we made holes and threaded the strings through. Then we had the first thrill of realising that this was our own gymkhana, when we could choose our own number, the one we liked best or thought was lucky for us. I chose 15 because it is a number I always like the look of, and John chose 7 which is supposed to be the luckiest number in the world, and Ann chose 21, and Mercy Dulbottle—who, strange as it may seem, was the fourth member of our party—shut her eyes and drew a number and it was 11, and she said it would do as well as any other as she hadn't the slightest chance of winning anything in any case.

John said that was the wrong attitude altogether, and it was known as a defeatist approach to life, and people with such an attitude shouldn't be in a riding club at all or enter for a gymkhana; and I said, "Shut up, John," because for one horrified moment I thought Mercy was going to weep. But she came round and said she hadn't meant it like that at all, and she knew that, thanks to Miss Durdon, she had a beautiful pony, and Miss Durdon herself had said that if Mercy would pull herself together and remember that she wasn't a human grasshopper but had hands and feet like any other rider, and would keep her head up and look as if she was enjoying herself, she might even get a few marks in the open horse-and-rider class.

At that moment there was a knock on the door. It was Stanley Trimble who had ridden over from the farm on his new pony, Peter, which I had helped him to buy. Stanley was now riding very well indeed, and I never saw so much improvement in anybody. This was partly because he was frightfully keen, and partly because he was the kind of person who never forgets a single thing he is told, so I never had to tell him twice.

Stanley said that the juniors had had a meeting, and had decided that for their competition they would like an obstacle race.

" Carry me out ! " said Ann. " You must enjoy getting hot."

" We thought it would be fun," said Stanley, " and take a long time. I hate those games where it is all over in about two minutes. We're going to have a pile of coats and caps and shoes at one end of the course, and you have to sort out your own and put them on, and you have to crawl through a drainpipe and call your pony to you at the other end, and then you have to eat a dry bun, and blindfold yourself and ride in and out of some bottles and if you touch one you have to go back to the beginning."

" And by the time you've all gone back to the beginning about ten times," said Ann, " that competition will have gone on for an hour and we'll all be bored stiff with watching you."

" Oh, let the kids have their own fun their own way,"

said John. " Personally I can't think of anything worse, but they'll think they're getting something."

" I hope we *are* getting something," said Stanley cheekily, " and I hope you're going to allocate some decent prizes for the junior events and not keep them all for yourselves, you big ones."

" Well, what do you want ? " said John, and Stanley said that he would like the first prize for the junior competition to be the box of stable equipment that Mrs. Darcy had given.

" I suppose we'd better let them have it," I said, " though those lovely brushes and clippers would have been nice for the senior jumping."

Meanwhile in spite of all the preparations for the gymkhana we had to keep up the ordinary activities of the riding club, so we planned a cross country ride for the following Tuesday.

" And that's the last big event we'll be able to have," I said, " because the Saturday after that is Chatton Show and we'll all have to practise."

Clarissa and Cecilia made rather a fuss when they discovered that the cross-country ride was to be just a ride, and did not involve water jumping and stone fences, but we managed to squash them by weight of numbers, and John pointed out that the younger ones had as much right to the fun as we had, and that people who wanted fancy prancing should enter for show events elsewhere.

" You needn't come if you don't want to," I said, but Clarissa and Cecilia were too afraid of missing something not to come.

" That's settled them," said John. " Nothing like taking a firm line."

" You'll be sorry," said Clarissa darkly, " if you take a pack of kids on a cross-country ride. However it's your funeral. I'm not in the least responsible."

The day of the ride was lovely. Blue sky, rolling white clouds, and enough breeze to make it exhilarating.

Ann came to call for me, and we rode slowly to the field where we were going to meet the rest, so as not to lather the ponies. When we arrived, there were Clarissa and Cecilia mounted looking very trim and wearing hard hats.

" Hullo, Jill," said my cousin. " Not got your hard hat on ? Bad example to the young ones. I was taught that you should always wear a hard hat on a cross-country ride."

I knew she was only baiting me, as I was dressed like everybody else, in shirt and jodhpurs, and no hat at all.

We started to round up the field, and found there were twenty-two of us, of whom eight were juniors ; and then I realised what Clarissa had meant, because most of the mothers of the eight juniors had turned up too, and were making a great fuss about how far were we going, and was it dangerous, and Hilda mustn't attempt to jump any water, and we simply must not go on any road at all because Richard's pony couldn't bear the sight of even the family car.

" Why did they come at all ? " I muttered angrily, and Clarissa overheard me and said, " I told you so ! "

John very patiently explained to all the mothers that we were going to ride across Neshbury Common, and through the pine woods, and along the edge of the Downs and back through the lanes, and it was all perfectly simple and straightforward, and anybody could drop out at any minute and go home if they wanted to ; whereupon some of the mothers said they would go in the car and meet us half-way.

"You see ? " said Clarissa, rolling her boiled goose-

berry eyes at John. "We haven't to go on the road, and we haven't to cross any water, or ride at any pace above a trot, and we're to be met half-way with smelling salts and bandages. What is this—a pram parade?"

Of course it wasn't really as bad as that. The juniors

were all as keen as mustard, once they got out of their fond mothers' clutches, and we all went cantering across Neshbury Common in the sunshine.

"When we get to the main road, everybody halt," I called back. "We've got to cross it to get to the woods. Pass the message back."

John and Clarissa galloped on ahead to get to the road first and make sure that everybody *did* halt, and it was just as well, because you could see the cars simply sizzling along the tarmac.

Everybody came to a very ragged halt. Two ponies reared, one girl fell off, and Alec Manston's pony turned and bolted.

Alec yelled, "Shan't be coming back. My pony won't cross the road, anyway. See you later." And that was the last we saw of Alec that day.

John stepped into the road and held up his hand to the traffic, like a traffic cop. Several lorries and cars stopped, I suppose from sheer curiosity to see what was coming, and the riding club began to cross. Some of the cautious ones dismounted and led their ponies, and some of us just rode, trying to look nonchalant, which wasn't easy as one lorry driver was yelling, "Tallyho, tallyho!" all the time, and a would-be funny man in a car shouted out, "Which way to the Derby?"

"I think all people who don't ride and haven't any manners ought to be massacred," said Diana, who was next to me, but I couldn't help giggling, it was so funny really.

Our one idea was to get the juniors across safely, and of course at the last minute Pam Derry's pony had to rear and stand on end, and a woman in a car began to shriek her head off, and Ann said to her sister, "You little drip ! " and Pam glared and got control of Buttons, and it was all over. We were on the other side.

" My gosh, what a good thing the fond mammas didn't see that bit ! " I said.

We rode along a rough, winding track, skirting the woods, and as we passed a group of cottages some men who were doing their gardens straightened up to wave at us. Then we came to the top of the hill, and there was a magnificent view ahead of us. It made you feel you could ride on for ever.

" There are some lovely steep banks about here," said John. " Couldn't we stop a minute and try some Italian cavalry stunts ? Now, you kids, you're not to do this."

He then shortened his stirrups, sat forward, and proceeded to slither down the bank. It looked rather exciting and showy, so we all tried it, only I don't suppose we looked a bit like Italian cavalry ; and when the juniors began to shriek, " Oh, you mean things ! Why can't we do it ? " we thought we had better stop and get on with the ride, rather than face the fond mammas with a lot of unconscious Bods.

Diana then suggested that we should go out of our way a bit, because there was a ruined castle about two miles away where she had once been taken for a picnic, and it was great fun and we could pretend to be a troop of horse clattering over the drawbridge, except that there wasn't a drawbridge nowadays because the moat wasn't a moat but just a grassy ditch.

We thought this was a good idea and we set off in an organised string, with Diana leading as she was supposed to know the way ; only we lost a bit of time because one of the juniors' ponies went lame with a stone in his

hoof, and we had to get down and give the aforesaid junior a lesson on how to get the stone out without hurting the pony, which I must say Clarissa did very deftly and quickly. I daresay I could have done it as deftly and quickly myself, only I didn't get the chance, and honour where honour is due.

We found the castle and clattered in through the massive arch. All that was left was a ring of broken walls round a turfy ward. The ponies liked it, and began to crop.

" Wouldn't this make a smashing place for circus practice ? " said somebody. " Let's ride them round like Liberty horses."

So we did that, and one or two of the boys tried circus tricks, like jumping off and on again at the canter, and the kids were most impressed ; but the ponies had soon had enough of this, so we left them cropping happily in the peaceful enclosure and began to explore the ruins.

We found a staircase leading up to what had been a room. There was still part of a fireplace there, and a big window embrasure with a stone seat all round.

" Oh, isn't it romantic ? " said my cousin Cecilia. " I can just picture the beautiful ladies in flowing martingales—— "

" Farthingales, you dope," said Clarissa.

" I mean those chiffon things they held their hats on with," said Cecilia indignantly.

" Simples," I said scornfully.

" Wimples, you drip," said Clarissa. " Simples are what they gave the knights when they had colic."

" I think you're all perfectly sordid," said Cecilia.

" I wonder what happened to the people who lived in this room ? "

" Murdered, I should think," said John. " They made a speciality of it in those days. I say, wouldn't it be smashing to stay here and camp ? We could make some sort of barrier across the gate to keep the ponies in, and we could build a fire in this hearth and cook sausages. Then we could pull some of the stones out and find buried treasure of ye olden tymes."

" More like some mouldy old buried bones," said David.

" Oh gosh ! " yelled Ann. " Have you looked at your watches ? We're about an hour late, and all those parents will be waiting at the end of the woods and thinking we're dead."

" To horse ! To horse ! " I yelled, and we all stampeded towards the ponies. It was fun. We all leapt into the saddles and went charging out of the main gate with such a din as you never heard, and just outside there was a very sedate picnic party who must have arrived after we went in.

They were practically terrified to death, thinking the Middle Ages had come to life again or something, so of course some of us had to go back and apologise.

" We're frightfully sorry if we scared you," I said. " We didn't know anybody would be there. There was nobody about when we went in."

The picnickers were quite ancient—about fifty years old I should think—but in spite of that they were quite intelligent and grasped the situation at once, and one of the men said, " I'm only too glad to see a crowd of young people engaged in such a healthy pastime as riding their ponies to visit a ruined castle. It takes me back to my childhood. Do you happen to be a riding club ? "

I said that was exactly what we were, and Ann with great presence of mind said, " Would you like to come to our gymkhana ? It's on Saturday week."

They all said they'd like nothing better than to come, and wouldn't fail to be there, so we told them where it was and rode off after the others.

" Nothing like improving the shining hour," said Ann.

I said, " The shining what ? " and she said, " Well, it's Shakespeare, or something. It means killing two birds with one stone."

By the time we caught the others up we were all terribly hot, and we proceeded to the woods at a walk that was practically a dawdle. We lolloped along the narrow track in single file, and gradually the shade of the pines closed in on us, and the ponies loved the feel of the soft turf under their feet, and there was a kind of mysterious feeling that is also adventurous ; you know what it is like riding through pine woods.

We went a bit out of our way again so that we could splash through a shallow pond, because everybody knows how lovely it is to ride through water, but of course a kid called Hilda Marshall had to skid and slither off her pony slap into what was only about six inches of water. It is surprising how wet you can get in six inches of water. Hilda looked as if she had been in the Atlantic for a week.

" There ! " said Diana. " Look at her. . . . And it was *her* mother who said we hadn't to jump any water."

" I haven't been jumping any water," said Hilda.

" Your mother will think you've been jumping the Thames," said John.

Hilda half began to cry, and then stopped and said, " Oh look ! Some of the others are jumping gorse bushes ! "

" Stop them ! " I said to John. " I don't care if they go home full of prickles, but *not* the ponies."

" Whoops ! " cried John, and raced after the others, flicking his riding stick at them and rounding them up.

" OOh ! " yelled Hilda. " Come quick, Gooseberry is sinking."

" You dope ! " I said. " Why didn't you lead him out at once ? "

There was poor Gooseberry, his eyes wild with fright, trying to heave himself the wrong way. John and I got hold of his head on either side, and began to work him back, and what with Gooseberry twisting and plunging and the slime popping and squelching we soon had as much wet on us as Hilda, who merely stood on the bank and said, " Oh dear, can't you get him out ? "

With a final heave out came the pony, and John and I fairly got christened with a shower of muddy water. Then we all sat down on the bank to have a rest.

" Now you can get some grass, Hilda," said John, " and jolly well clean up your own disgusting pony."

Hilda got a wisp of grass and transferred some of the green slime from Gooseberry to her own jodhpurs, and said, " Blow ! That's all I'm going to do. We're frightfully late. Mummy will be having a fit."

So we collected the rest of the crowd and got back to the woods. It wasn't much cooler among the close-growing pines, and there were more flies than you would have imagined could exist in the whole of England.

I suppose I was riding along in a sort of trance.
Anyway, I never even saw the branch that hit me.
Suddenly everything began to whirl round, I let out
one yell, and after that I don't remember anything
much except a lot of confusion.

Somehow I wasn't riding through the pinewoods

any more. I thought I was dreaming. I decided it
was time I woke up. So I did, and I was in bed at
home.

I said, " Golly, what's the time ? "

Mummy, who was standing by the window, said,
" So you're awake at last ? There's not much the
matter with you, only you knocked yourself right out.
In pine woods you should really either look where you're
going, or wear a hard hat."

K

I blinked, and said, " Did I really take a toss ?   How did I get home ? "

" Somebody's mother very kindly brought you in a car."

" What day is it ? " I said.

" Oh, it's still the same day," said Mummy laughing. " It happened about two hours ago. The doctor's coming to look at you again, and I expect he'll keep you in bed for a few days."

Honestly, I felt as if I'd been sentenced to six months in the salt mines.

" But I can't ! " I yelled.   " It's Chatton Show on Saturday, and I'm going to ride Mrs. Darcy's Messmate in the Grade C jumping, and I want to do about three days' hard practice."

Mummy shrugged her shoulders and said, " I'm afraid it's just too bad," and I lay there fretting and fuming. Was there ever such awful luck ?   The year before I was out of the Chatton Show because I sprained my wrist, and now once more Doom had overtaken me.

" I'm perfectly all right," I grumbled.   " I'm going to get up."

" Not till the doctor has seen you," said Mummy in a voice that sounded like iron chains clanking together. " By the way, there are about nine of your friends waiting outside to hear how you are.   I'll tell them you're becoming quite yourself again."

" Tell them I'm going mad," I said gloomily.   " I shall, if I can't ride on Saturday."

The doctor came about an hour later.   I was sitting up eating an enormous supper of crab sandwiches, ice-cream, chocolate cake and coffee. He tapped my back and head all over, and as there were no hideous grinding noises of broken bones he said, "No harm done. Just a few days nice rest, young lady, and you'll be as good as new."

I said miserably, "A few more days nice rest and there'll be plenty of harm done, because I'll be biting people and smashing up the furniture," and he said, "What's the trouble?" and I told him about Chatton Show and the Grade C jumpimg.

"Tch! Tch!" he said. "You horsy people! You're not made like ordinary human beings. I remember a woman I used to attend a few years ago. Dislocated collar-bone and concussion on the Wednesday, and on the Saturday she was riding in a point-to-point and seemed all the better for it."

"That's wonderful," I said. "That's all I wanted."

"Oh dear," he said. "I shouldn't have said that. Whatever will your mother think? I'd better tell her you're to stay in bed a week, with your door locked."

"Be a sport!" I said, grinning at him. "I know I'll be okay, if I can only get up. I'm frightfully tough, honestly I am."

He said, "Let me see, when's the show? Saturday? And it's Tuesday now. You can get up on Thursday, and no riding before Friday, do you hear?"

"Friday? Oh, please make it Thursday," I implored. "I must have two days' practice."

"*Friday*," he repeated firmly. "And one more squeak out of you and I'll lock your door myself and give your mother the key."

Wednesday felt much like being in prison, and every moment seemed an hour; but in the afternoon Mrs. Darcy came round and we talked about the show.

"You'll be quite all right," she said. "You can

take it easy, because it will be Messmate's first big competition and I don't expect much from him.   It's just
the experience.   He's a nice ride, and very sensible.
Come round tomorrow, and even if you can't ride you
can watch me put him round the practice jumps and
get an idea how he goes."

This brightened life for me considerably.   The next
morning, if Mummy had any ideas of me enjoying some
more nice rest and breakfast in bed she was disappointed
because I was up and dressed in shirt and jodhs before
she was downstairs.   I did this in case she stopped
me.

By nine o'clock I was round at Mrs. Darcy's, and
found her lunging a pony.

She said, " Back on your feet again ?   Good for you.
Feeling a bit rocky ? "

As a matter of fact I was, but I didn't want to admit
it.   She asked how many events I was entered for at
Chatton Show, and I said six.   She said, what about
cutting everything but the Grade C jumping, and I
gave a yell of dismay and said, " Oh help, it's not as
bad as that ! "   I was particularly keen on the under-
sixteen jumping and I didn't want to disappoint Rapide
in this, so in the end we decided that I would do the
two jumping competitions and cut out the other events.
Fate seemed to have a down on me as regards Chatton
Show so I thought I'd better be cautious, especially as
I hadn't done the Grade C jumping before, but Messmate was a nice friendly bay gelding who knew me well
and was very co-operative.   Not a horse with a great
deal of imagination or initiative, but most willing and
quick to respond and a light, neat jumper.

I spent most of Friday morning round Mrs. Darcy's

jumps, and in the afternoon she let me bring Rapide and practise him too. By then I felt as if my legs were bending under me and I had quite a headache, but of course I kept quiet about these trifles.

CHAPTER XII

Me—And Grade C

WHEN I got home Ann was there. " I say ! " she said. " You did take a toss. We all thought you'd get into the papers, but you didn't. Mummy was so unnerved by your accident that she went out and bought me three hard hats, and in future I think she'll expect me to wear them one on top of the other. Have you got a huge bump ? "

I told her that my bump had been practically as big as a tennis ball, but it was now fading away.

" I never heard what happened at the end of the ride," I said, and she said that nothing much else had happened, the parents had all been waiting at the end of the woods, but what with me and my toss everything else had paled into insignificance.

Unfortunately we got a poor day for Chatton Show, one of those days when you don't know what the weather is going to do. By noon it had settled down to a messy drizzle. It meant wet macks and wet ponies, and we spent most of the waiting time eating Mars bars and trying to keep ourselves and our ponies reasonably tidy.

The grass of course was sopping wet and the take-offs were greasy. In the under-sixteen jumping I was lucky enough to ride second, before the take-offs were reduced to actual mud. Rapide was in very good form. As soon as I felt him increase speed of his own accord for the first jump I knew he was going to have a

decent round. This was important to me, as it was my
first year in the senior event. I hadn't hoped to be in
the first three, but at the same time didn't want to
disgrace myself. To my delight I got off with four
faults—which considering the state of the ground was
little short of miraculous, only Rapide had always liked
soft going.

As we rode out of the ring Rapide half turned his
head to me and I saw he was giving me his smug smile
which meant, There you are ! You didn't think I'd
be so good, did you ? "

Nobody did a clear round. Two boys tied with two
faults each and jumped off for first and second, and to
my amazement I was placed third. I have never been
so thrilled as I was to receive the yellow rosette.

In the other events our riding club members showed

up well. John Watson won a senior showing class,
Alec Manston a best pony class, David Neville won the
junior jumping and another of our members was second,
Val and Jack Heath won the teams competition, and
several other people got prizes in the competitions.

I must say when it was time for the Grade C jumping
I had chunks of qualms. Cold shivers ran up and down
my spine when we were called into the collecting ring.

" Go on with you ! " said Mrs. Darcy, slapping Messmate's slightly wet flank. " Keep calm, Jill, this is
nothing at all. I only want Messmate to get the show-
ring experience, and he's so sensible he won't play you
up or run out or anything. He'll just go on jumping."

" I don't want to let you down," I mumbled.

" Don't be an idiot," she laughed. " Go on. You're
riding seventh."

I watched a young farmer called Knowles ride to the
start at the far end of the ring. The first jump was a
brush fence, then there was a stile, a wall, an in-and-out,
a gate and a triple bar.

The rain had stopped by now and there was a drying
wind. They had put down a lot of sawdust at the take-
offs, and Billy Knowles's horse loathed the sight of it.
He refused at each of the first three jumps, and finally
knocked the gate over and ran out of the ring. This
wasn't a very encouraging sight for me. The next three
competitors also had a bad time, and I thought, three
refusals at the first jump is probably what I'll get, and
that'll be the end of me.

Then a woman called Standish did a clear round.

" Help ! " I said. " She must be exceptional with
the grass in this state."

" It's what I expected," said Mrs. Darcy. " She's

particularly good, with years of experience, but she never enters a horse that she isn't sure of. It's silly, really. I mean, Grade C jumping is meant to bring on and encourage horses, and even if you've got a bit of a dud you ought to give him a chance by riding in a

decent event. Messmate is far from a dud. He's going to enjoy himself and so are you."

By the time my number was called I was thinking of something else, and had to be called twice. I could see the judge glowering at me and thought, well this isn't too good a start! However, to my delight Messmate took charge, and before I knew where I was we were cantering away to the first jump, and over he popped, so easily that I hardly noticed it.

I never knew such a horse for enjoying himself. By the time we were in and out of the in-and-out I began to enjoy myself too, and though we came to grief at the triple bar and collected six faults, I felt very pleased with the round as a whole.

"Jolly good," said Mrs. Darcy. "You were both a bit over-excited by the time you got to that last jump, that was all that was the matter with you."

Ann rode up and said, "Gosh! I nearly thought you were going to do a clear round. The first five jumps were supersonic; Messmate had inches to spare. He's going to make a great jumper, Mrs. Darcy."

"Yes," she said, "he's surprised even me. I'll be riding him in the open jumping some day. And Jill handled him really well."

"Fluke!" I said modestly. We all petted and flattered Messmate, and waited for the rest of the competitors to finish.

"You've got a chance," Ann said. "Apart from Mrs. Standish nobody has got less than six faults."

"You spoke too soon," Mrs. Darcy said, as a storm of clapping broke out. "There goes Meg Wilson with only four faults."

I was so sure by now that I was out of it that I didn't pay much attention, and before I knew it they were calling in the winners.

"Twenty-nine, eleven, and nineteen," said Ann, and then shrieked, "Nineteen! That's you, Jill."

"What about it?" I said.

"They've called you in, you dope."

I rode in, feeling like a dream, and found that another competitor had also got six faults and we had to ride it off over three jumps. He got a clear three, and I got two faults at the wall. It was entirely my own fault and not Messmate's, and I was furious with myself, because it is a failing of mine that if anything depends on a certain jump that's the one I muff. However I was reserve, and got a certificate, and everybody was thrilled about it, particularly Mrs. Darcy.

I said, " I could kick myself. I had to go and put on pressure at the wall, and if I'd left it to the horse he'd have been over like a bird."

Ann said, " You've done jolly well, so now you can come and watch me make a mess of the bending race."

" Don't be silly," I said, " you'll win it hands down. It's an art, the way you do a bending race, there's nobody in the county to touch you at it."

Ann won her heat quite easily, and also the semi-finals. By the time the final came up the four ponies who were racing were all hot and excited, and there was some plunging and bucking. The judge, who was one of those impatient types, got annoyed and kept yelling No ! Ann's pony thought he said Go, and off she went, only to be called back, while the judge was purple. However the four of them finally got off at a tremendous gallop and went down the line of poles like lightning, so fast in fact that at the turn one of them went straight on and was seen no more. Ann took the turn with an expertness which it was a joy to watch, and though the other girl was a neck ahead Ann caught up and there was an apparently dead heat finish.

" They're going to have some fun sorting that one out," said John Watson who was watching with me. " It's a real photo finish, and I doubt if they'll make them ride it off again."

However they did, and in the midst of thunderous cheers Ann remained as cool as a cucumber and won by a head.

When she joined us she said, " Honestly, I don't remember a thing about that race.   I never rode so fast
in my life.   It was like being swept away by a whirl-
wind.   Wasn't George marvellous ? " she added, leading
her pony away to rub him down.

Then we all went to watch the open jumping, which
I need not describe as you have all seen open jumping
so many times you know exactly what it is like.   When

you see such wonderful riding it makes you feel that you
know nothing and are less than the dust.

I went home with two rosettes, a certificate, £1, and
a clothes brush with a leather back, which was so much
more than I'd expected that I felt quite light-headed.

In the evening Mrs. Darcy came round with a box of
chocolates for me.

" Oh no," I said.   " You shouldn't.   It was enough
of a treat to be able to ride Messmate in the competition."

"Go on," she said. "You've earned it. You got more out of Messmate than anybody else could have done. By the way," she went on, "I hear good opinions on all sides about this riding club of yours. I think it's been a really good thing for the neighbourhood."

I said I didn't know about that, and I had even had moments when I thought the riding club nothing but a menace, but certainly everybody had improved since they joined.

"The work you've put in is a credit to you," she said.

"Oh gosh, no !" I said. "Not me. Some of the others have worked as hard or harder. John and Diana and Val have given up loads of their time, and even so the whole thing would have been a flop if it hadn't been for Captain Cholly-Sawcutt and Mr. Storm and Miss Durdon and Major Hooley taking an interest."

Mrs. Darcy said that was the beauty of riding, experts being so willing to help the young ones, and if they weren't willing they had no right to call themselves riders at all, and I said, How true.

Just then about five people from the riding club turned up, and we all had coffee and discussed the show, and said how good it was that our members had done so well because it would make people think that our gymkhana was going to be worth attending.

"And I jolly well hope it will be ! " I added.

When Monday came we were all so up to the eyes in preparations for our own gymkhana the following Saturday that we had forgotten Chatton Show. The field became a scene of furious activity as everybody practised for their events. There was Miss Durdon

looking very intense and simply bursting with energy
as she schooled Mercy, for she was determined that
Mercy should win *something*. In the end we had to
stick in an extra class, just to please Miss Durdon.
This was an open class and consisted of riding round the
perimeter of the ring at a collected walk, and it was of
course designed especially for Mercy to shine. Actually
we couldn't think of anything duller to do, or deadlier
to watch, but we had to give in to Miss Durdon. Unfortunately only eight people, including Mercy, entered
for it, and the others were small juniors which was going
to make poor Mercy look more like a grasshopper than
ever.

"Look," said Diana, "we can't leave the poor dope
like that. Let's be noble and enter for it. Come on,
Jill—you and I and John will enter, that'll make it look
better, and what about you, Clarissa? You're big. It
won't kill you."

"Okay," said Clarissa who was in an obliging mood.
"Cecilia can come in too. We'll all lollop round, and
Mercy is sure to win, and we'll call it the Creeping
Race."

So we put it down on the schedule directly before tea,
because we guessed by then that nobody would stop to
watch it and we would get it over painlessly.

We were very pleased that the entries for all the
events were pouring in, and everybody in the village
seemed to be coming to watch. We were charging 6d.
for entrance, half price for under-fourteen, and one-
and-six for tea and cakes, so we looked like making a
lot of money after expenses were paid, and this we were
of course going to give to animal charities.

I started having frightful dreams at night. One was

that on the day the gymkhana field was all covered with snow ; another was that Black Boy turned into a giraffe as I was riding him into the ring ; another was that nobody came to the gymkhana and John Watson said we would have to eat fifty cakes each to get rid of them. I thought these dreams were rather unique, but when I told the others they said that they themselves had much more spectacular and appalling ones before which my own paled ; in fact Diana Bush had dreamed that when we started to ride everything went into slow motion and got slower and slower until it stopped and there we all were glued to the ground, and John Watson said he had dreamed that Captain Cholly-Sawcutt turned into a black panther and ate all the ponies, only I didn't believe that one, I was sure he had made it up.

Then of course we were convinced it was going to pour with rain on the day. But it didn't. It was a very decent sort of day, not too hot, with some sun and some cloud and a nice breeze blowing from the north-west.

But I'm going too far ahead.

On the Thursday Clarissa Dandleby said, " It's time we got these kids together and gave them a briefing about turning out decent on Saturday. We don't want any pink shirts and orange ties, and they might not even be *clean.*"

" That would be *lamentable* ! " said Diana, copying Clarissa's voice.

Clarissa was mad, and said very snootily, " Just for that you can lecture them yourself. I couldn't care less what they look like. I shall enjoy myself on Saturday and feel *no* responsibility at all."

" Oh, don't be such a wet drip," said John. " I'll

get the kids together and brief them. I think the best thing to do is to tell them that anybody who turns up on Saturday looking grubby, or with a dirty pony, just won't be allowed to ride."

" I say ! That's a bit drastic," I said. " It would quite likely be May Cholly-Sawcutt. You know what she is."

" All the better," said John. " I'm sure it's what her father would wish."

So we got everybody together and John laid down the law about clean people, clean clothes, and clean ponies and tack.

" And no pink shirts with orange ties," finished Diana.

" Who on earth would come in a pink shirt with an orange tie ? " said one of the juniors.

" I don't know," said Diana innocently. " It was Clarissa's idea."

Clarissa glared, and it was all rather funny, because a rumour went round that Clarissa had intended to ride in a pink shirt with an orange tie and had been suppressed at the last minute, and practically everybody in the village got hold of this story—which took a lot of living down, as Clarissa found out later.

The night before the gymkhana we went up to Miss Durdon's—by invitation—to check over and allocate the prizes. She was as keen as mustard, and had added a few prizes off her own bat, which was very decent of her. In fact, we began to realise that we owed a lot to Miss Durdon and it was a good job we had let her be President of the Riding Club. So I thought it was up to me to express this in rather shaky words, which I did, and the others clapped. Miss Durdon snorted with pleasure, and in came Mercy pushing the trolley with coffee and chocolate éclairs, which was just the finishing touch.

" We've just been telling Miss Durdon that we think that everything she's done is pretty terrific," said John.

" Oh dear, I do hope I'm going to win something tomorrow," said Mercy despondently, " but I'm quite sure I shan't and I shall be so humiliated."

" Bosh ! " said John. " That's not the right attitude at all, is it, Miss Durdon ? You ought to visualise yourself sailing over everything and carrying home all the prizes. That's called psychology."

" I jolly well hope Mercy isn't going to be as psychological as all that," said Ann. " Some of the rest of us might like a few prizes." Whereupon Miss Durdon told us a long and rambling story about how she had once won an open jumping competition in India just by visualising herself soaring over everything, and I began to wonder if there was anything in it, and if so, what a good thing everybody didn't try it.

" What about going down to the field to see what's happening there ? " said John. So we all went down— including Miss Durdon and Mercy—and there was Mr. Trimble and two or three other men, putting up the ropes for the ring and the forms for the spectators to sit on, and the tea marquee, and the smaller tent for the iudges.

Mr. Trimble said it was surprising to him how much interest our riding club gymkhana had aroused in the surrounding countryside, and everybody for miles round was going to be there, from what he'd heard.

I said, well in that case the few seats we'd got were

L

going to be nothing at all ; and he said, mark his words, they'd be standing ten deep.

Ann said she thought that was wildly exaggerated, as with all the superior horsy events that were being held everywhere in August, why should people bother about a potty little affair like ours, that didn't mean much to anybody but us ? And Mr. Trimble said very darkly, " You'll see."

CHAPTER XIII

The Big Day

I HAVE always been told you ought to get to bed early the night before a gymkhana, but it didn't happen to me this time, because somebody—I don't remember who—said at the last minute, "Shouldn't we have some notices stuck about the roads saying *This Way to the Gymkhana*? The field isn't too easy to find."

This threw us all into a flap. John said, "People can ask, can't they?" and Ann said, "They won't bother. If they can't find it they'll go home."

We had some cardboard and Indian ink left over, so in the end we started doing some rather sploshy notices, *This Way To The Gymkhana*, and although it was practically dark by then we went out on bikes and nailed these up to trees at the corners of the lanes that led to the gymkhana field. Ann said, "It's probably illegal, and the farmers will pull them down tomorrow morning and sue us for something-or-other;" however by then we were too tired to care, and the farmers didn't pull the notices down so perhaps it was worth while.

I got home at 11 p.m. and Mummy was waiting for me brandishing an axe, so to speak. She said she had been waiting for me for two hours, and she never heard of such a thing, and it was time I stopped all this riding club nonsense if this was what it led to, and so on. I

said I was frightfully sorry, and explained about the notices at the last minute, and she calmed down, but the atmosphere wasn't sympathetic. I was starving too, so I went in the kitchen and ate everything that was lying about and made a jug of cocoa, and it was nearly midnight when I finally went upstairs and set my alarm clock for six a.m.

It seemed as if I had hardly got into bed before that alarm went off. I couldn't believe it was six o'clock, but it was. I felt very bleary-eyed and wobbly-kneed, and the chilly dawn didn't appeal to me at all. My spirits were at their lowest ebb—as it says in books—and I was sure the gymkhana was going to be a flop.

I put on a sweater and my dungarees and looked out of the window. The eastern sky was brightening and there was a kind of shining mist over everything ; the air smelt good. It was going to be a fine day, and whatever kind of a fool I made of myself it didn't matter, the gymkhana was going to be all right.

I flew downstairs and made a cup of tea and rushed out to the stable. I fed the ponies and left them with their feeds and buckets of water while I dashed round collecting the grooming tools and the soap flakes for their tails. Soon excitement seized me and I began to whistle. I worked like mad, and after about two hours the grooming was all finished and the ponies looked lovely. Black Boy looked like polished ebony, and Rapide gleamed in the sunlight and his tail was like an advertisement for somebody's shampoo.

I heard Mummy calling that breakfast was ready, and my heart went down with a honk of shame, because I really had intended to take her up a cup of tea but I just hadn't noticed how the time was going. Now I shouldn't get any credit at all for my good intentions. I went in and had porridge and bacon and egg, and I said I would make my own sandwiches to take with me for lunch. Although the gymkhana didn't begin till half-past one, we were all going to be at the field early in the morning for last minute arrangements and to see that everything was O.K.

I put on my jodhpurs that were just back from the cleaners, and a clean brown shirt, fawn tie, and black velvet cap. I polished my boots madly and hoped everybody else was doing the same. I pushed the polish and the rags into my saddle-bag in case any of the younger ones hadn't bothered. In any case, we should all want a rub up before we rode. I knew I should forget something, and it turned out to be a clean handkerchief, but Mummy ran after me with one.

"Do get down early," I said to her. "I'll try and keep you a seat in a good place by putting my saddle-bag on it, but you know what people are if there's a crowd."

I wasn't by any means the first at the field. I suppose everybody else was excited too and wanted to be at the scene of action. Mr. Trimble was still working away, making everything trim.

"Gosh, do you suppose he's been here all night?" said Ann. "It nearly looks like it. After all he's done, I can't help hoping that Stanley wins a prize of some sort."

As the members of the riding club appeared we checked them off to see they were clean and dressed properly, and that their ponies were O.K. Then we tethered all the ponies in a row under the trees at the far side of the field. The whole set-up looked quite professional, and I was delighted ; the ring and the seats, the tea tent and the judges' tent, and away at one side the beautiful freshly-painted jumps.

"I've got the final list of entries," said John Watson, coming up. "Lots of people I never heard of."

"Help !" said Val Heath, reading over his shoulder. "Half those people do nothing but go round riding in all the gymkhanas, and winning everything. We'll be lucky if we stand a chance at all."

"Never mind," said Diana ironically. "We'll get a nice ride."

Just then Clarissa and my cousin Cecilia appeared. They looked terrific. Both were attired as though to ride with the Queen, in black coats, hard hats, cream cord breeches, and brilliantly polished boots that made

your eyes ache to look at them. They both had powder
and lipstick on and looked hard and experienced and
about twenty-one.

" Crumbs ! " said John. " Are you women looking
for the Royal enclosure ? "

" I say, Cecilia ! " I said. " You look just like a film
star. Even if none of us win anything you'll give tone
to the party."

" If I were you," said Ann, " I'd get those saddles off
and the ponies parked under the trees or they'll be in
a worse sweat than ever when it's time to ride."

They cantered away, and John said, " We ought to
have those two at the gate to lure people in. They'd
certainly make it look like a supersonic gymkhana."

At last we were satisfied that everything was ready,
and while we were gobbling up our sandwiches a lot of
spectators began to arrive and find seats, and the non-
riding club entries began to pour in, all looking frightfully superior and riding the most competent-looking
ponies I ever saw.

" Oh, why did we start this ? " I said to Ann.
" Shan't we look small if nobody in the riding club wins
anything ?   It could easily happen."

Ann just shrugged her shoulders and said, " Kismet,
it is the will of Allah."

At last everything was ready, the seats were packed
and people were standing up all round. The judges
were in their tent, and had been joined by Miss Durdon
who was a self-appointed judge, but nobody could very
well tell her not to be. The first class, the under-tens
showing-class, was ready to go into the ring, surrounded
by anxious mothers and cool-looking nannies telling
them how sweet they looked. Then they rode in, led

by a very fat little boy on a Shetland. Behind him was Pam Derry.

"Oh, for goodness' sake, look at Pam," said Ann crossly. "She's gazing round and grinning at everybody she knows. She's got simply no ring technique at all, and I told her fifty times to look straight between her pony's ears and remember where she is. She'll be disqualified in a minute and I'll die of shame."

There were several very dressed-up children holding their ponies on much too tight a rein, and one or two small ones who just sat on their ponies in a dazed sort of way and couldn't be said to be riding at all. The one I liked best—hoping I wasn't prejudiced—was a child called Paul Carris who belonged to the riding club. He was only eight and just about our youngest member, and he really rode very nicely, letting his pony walk out and then collecting him as he had been taught. When told to trot he was one of the few who did so. Some of them merely went on walking, some turned round and tried to go the other way, throwing the rest into wild confusion, one child burst into tears and fled to its nannie, and others' ponies began to crop grass. The judges looked a bit nonplussed, and Mrs. Darcy said loudly, "Walk! Walk!"

Nobody took much notice, so I suppose the judges thought the best thing was to start calling in.

Paul Carris was called in first, then a rather haughty-looking little girl I didn't know, who did everything correctly in a very dollish way, and third was Pam Derry who had at last come to her senses and showed a bit of control over her pony. The rest found their own places, except for those who had already given up and gone out of the ring.

The judges examined the ponies, and Pam behaved very smartly, so that the judges went into a huddle and you could tell they were considering whether to put her in second place ; however they didn't, and simply doled out the rosettes, red for Paul, blue for the doll-girl, and yellow for Pam.

I was so thrilled at this good beginning, with two prizes for the riding club already, that I shrieked out Hurrah, and Clarissa who was passing said " What manners ! "

Ann said gloomily, " We'll never hear the end of this from Pam, and quite honestly she was only the best of a bad bunch."

" Never mind," I said.   " It's two rosettes for the riding club and we mightn't have got any."

The next event was the under-tens musical chairs— or sacks—and this was fun to watch. Most of the children behaved quite well, until seven or eight were left in and then they got over-excited and began to snatch sacks away from people who had claimed them. One girl rushed out weeping and the judges sent a boy off the field.   Finally there were four very tough-looking small boys left in—none of them members of the riding school, and they fought out the finish rather murderously.   Several mothers who were standing near me began to say it wasn't fair, and I thought it was a good thing when that particular event was over.

The under-fourteen showing class came next, and I was very anxious about this because half the entries were riding club members, and I felt it was important that we should make a good show here.

" I say, it'll look grim if we don't win anything here," said John Watson coming up to me.   " It'll look as if we hadn't taught them anything. There's a lot of opposition," he went on, as the class began to ride into the ring. "That kid at the front, I don't know who she is, but she looks pretty good."

She was a very pale, neat girl on a blood pony, and she rode with terrifying technique and efficiency and looked as if she spent her whole life doing this kind of thing at gymkhanas. Behind her came Hilda Marshall, one of our members, forgetting everything she had been taught, sitting too far back and sticking her legs out, and I gave a faint moan. David Neville came next, looking cool but a bit too self-conscious ; and then a very smart boy on a pony that was much too big for him. He gave his pony one or two whacks as he rode and some mammas who were standing near said, "That's a marvellous little rider, just look at him."

"Our members look much too stiff," said Ann. "I hope the judges won't think we taught them to ride like that."

"Oh, they don't look too bad," said John, "they'll relax in a minute. Look at this bunch meandering round—I'm glad they're not our members."

It was a very big class, with thirty-five entries, but you could see that about twenty of them weren't much good. Among these were some of our own members who through nerves or carelessness weren't doing themselves justice.

"Oh, look at June Cholly-Sawcutt !" said Diana. "She's crowding the pony in front—she's passing— why will she do these awful things ? She'll be disqualified in a minute."

"Yes, but May is riding quite nicely for once," I

said. " And she's gone into her canter just like I told her ! Good for May ! "

The canter was quite a test and weeded out the riders. One or two came off, one pony ran out, and the very smart boy was told off for using his stick. I counted five people on the wrong leg, and one hanging on to his pony's mane.

When the judge began to call in I was so anxious I shut my eyes.

" Tell me," I said to Ann. " I can't bear it."

" You'll pass right out when I tell you," said Ann. " May Cholly-Sawcutt is in second place. The first and third are strangers. David Neville is fourth and Stanley Trimble fifth."

I opened my eyes, and she was telling the truth.

I held my breath when May was told to lead her pony out, but she did it correctly. The test was the usual figure of eight. As if by magic May remembered to do it slowly and to change legs properly. David Neville's pony was a bit nappy and he didn't collect well. Stanley Trimble looked stiff and was frightfully pale, but his pony Peter behaved like an old hand. They all dismounted and took off their saddles while the judges examined the ponies.

" Oh, I hope May's is clean ! " I breathed, hardly daring it would be. But it must have been, because the judges made no alteration in the order except to change David and Stanley, so that Stanley was fourth and got the white rosette. While the prize-winners were cantering round the ring we all clapped and cheered like mad. I was better pleased than if I'd won a prize myself. May Cholly-Sawcutt simply lost her head and galloped madly, waving her rosette above her head and

yelling, " I've got a prize, I've got a prize, Daddy !
Daddy, look at me, I've got a prize ! "

Yes, Captain Cholly-Sawcutt himself was there, and
believe me he was nearly weeping.   If you can imagine
a member of the British Show Jumping team being all

of a dither at a kids' gymkhana, this was it.   He came
up to me and said in a dazed sort of way, " My daughter's
got a prize.   A second prize in a showing class.   My
hopeless, ham-handed daughter !   I've never been so
excited in my life.   And look how badly she's behaving
now, she'll cover me with shame."

" She was jolly good," I said.   " I knew one of the
girls would do well some day."

" I'll buy her as many ices as she wants," he said.
" She can have fifteen if she wants them.   I don't care
if she bursts now.   This is the greatest day of my life,
including the day we won the European Championship."

The next minute my hand was seized and wrung
until I yelled.   It was Mr. Trimble.   He was so choking
with pride over Stanley's reserve that he couldn't speak
at all.   It was rather funny, all these proud fathers, but
it did speak well for the riding club.

The next event was the under-fourteen obstacle race
which was run off in heats.   It was the hottest thing
I ever saw in my life.   The juniors had organised it
themselves and had put in everything they could think
of.   They had to ride to a pile of clothes and shoes and
sort out their own and put them on, they had to crawl
through drain-pipes, ride sitting backwards in the
saddle, eat a dry bun, whistle a tune, and finish up by
riding blindfold without knocking down bottles.   It
went on for ages, but the juniors didn't seem to care
though most of them looked as if they were going to
burst into flames.   The whole thing was won by Stanley
Trimble—Mr. Trimble was by now roaring his head off
with excitement—second was a stranger, and third a
girl called Poppy French, who didn't belong to the riding
club.

The next thing was Miss Durdon's special prize, the
parade round the ring at a collected walk, to give Mercy
a chance to win something.   Only twelve people had
bothered to enter for this, and they were all members
of the riding club.   It was the one that Clarissa had
called the Creeping Race, and she and Cecilia, John,

Diana and I were all in it, so as not to make it too tame
and hurt Miss Durdon's feelings. Mercy's pony was
so beautiful that the judges didn't look any further.
He arched his neck and his lovely tail blew in the breeze.
Mercy was neat and well turned out, and she sat up
straight and kept her hands down, and the collected
walk was just her cup of tea. She won it, of course, but
after it was over she came up to me and began to weep.

She said, " It was beastly. It looked as if I was
showing off, just to get a prize. I wish I hadn't entered
for it."

" Don't be silly, Mercy," I said. " You were much
the best and you deserved the prize."

" Do you really think I did ? " she said, brightening
up.

" Yes, you did. You earned it. You don't think
judges like Mrs. Darcy and Mr. Heath would have let
you have it just to please Miss Durdon if you didn't
deserve it ? "

That satisfied her, and we were all quite pleased she
had got a prize, because she was an awfully decent sort
really and very well-meaning, if dim.

By now of course all the spectators were thinking of
nothing but refreshments, and flocking to the tea tent
where Mrs. Watson was presiding over a long table
simply piled up with homemade cakes and buns and
biscuits. We all followed, and it was a thoroughly
happy jam. People kept coming and telling me they
thought the gymkhana was a jolly good show ; Captain
Cholly-Sawcutt was still rambling on about May being
second in the showing class (which naturally he couldn't
get over, neither could anybody else) and May was there
actually wearing her rosette *on her hair*. Clarissa Dandle-

by was glaring at her and muttering, What frightfully
bad form, but May couldn't care less.   Stanley Trimble's father and mother were holding a kind of reception
in one corner, with Stanley very blushing and embar-
rassed between them, and looking at John Watson as if
to say, Do come and rescue me ; but John just grinned
and walked away to where the ices were being sold.

Ann and I worked our way at last to the counter
and bought cakes, lemonade, and ice cream ; then we
fought out way out and sat under the trees near the
ponies.

"It's jolly good," I said.   "Better than I hoped.
The riding club has already got two prizes in the under-
ten showing class, two in the under-fourteen, as well as
Stanley's obstacle race and Mercy's creeping race prize.
I'm awfully glad Paul Carris won the under-tens, he's
such a nice kid."

Ann began to giggle, and said that there was something funny about Stanley Trimble and May Cholly-
Sawcutt and Mercy Dulbottle being the ones to cover
the riding club with glory in the early events, the very
last people you'd have thought of, and she hoped it
wasn't an omen.

I said, "An omen what of ? "   And Ann said, "It
would look frightful if nothing went as we expected the
whole afternoon and we made a flop in the major events
like the jumping."

"You would think of that," I said.   "Don't put me
off."

"You've simply got to win the senior jumping, Jill,"
she said, and I said, "Don't be silly.   How could I
when there'll be at least nine other people much better
than me ? "

Ann said she hoped that if I didn't win it John Watson would, and she could bear even Clarissa to win it rather than somebody who didn't belong to the riding club.

CHAPTER XIV

The Last Parade

THE jumps were all put up, and the junior entry was riding into the ring to inspect them, twenty-seven entries in all, fifteen of them members of the riding club.

We were standing by the rails looking at them with anxious critical eyes.

"Our main hopes," said John, "are David Neville and Alec Manston. I don't think the rest of our bunch stand much chance against outside opposition. There are some kids there who've won jumping competitions for miles around."

"It all depends on David's timing," I said. "Some days he times quite brilliantly and other days he's hopeless, and the worst of it is that on the days when he knows he isn't timing well he won't leave it to his pony, but presses. He isn't awfully reliable."

"I've just given him a good briefing," said John, "but I thought he was a bit too cocksure. Alec looks steady enough, but I'm afraid he's nervous. He hasn't had an awful lot of show experience, and though he jumps very well at practice it's a different thing in the ring with masses of people watching you."

As Alec led his pony round the jump which was nearest to us he smiled at us and we said, "Good luck, Alec!" John said, "Let her go, boy, and don't tighten up."

The first competitor into the ring was a farmer's daughter called Betty Prince who seemed to spend her whole life riding at pony shows. Wherever you went you saw Betty and her pony Blue Ticket. Blue Ticket had been an expensive pony and was a born jumper, and though Betty was rather an uninspired type of rider she had the sense to do everything correctly and leave the rest to her pony. Also, she never seemed to have any nerves.

Betty jumped a clear round without any apparent difficulty and rode out amid clapping.

" Well, that sets the standard ! " said John with a whistle.

The next competitor was a stranger to us, a boy on a grey pony that was too big for him. He took the first three jumps much too fast, crashed the fourth, and ran out. Then came a small girl called Lassie Perritt, who went round so slowly that we thought every minute she would be disqualified. I suppose she just got round in the allotted time, but she had fourteen faults.

The next three riders we were interested in, because they were our own members, but alas, they didn't do very well, getting six to eight faults each. Then came a very competent and experienced boy who was just on the verge of being out of the junior class and had won a lot of prizes. He got a clear round.

" David and Alec have got to be awfully good ! " groaned John. " Oh, here comes David."

It appeared to be one of David's good days; he took the first two jumps beautifully.

" Legs ! Legs ! " breathed John as David flashed by us. " Oh, he's too fast—too fast—he's going to lose his head—there you are ! "

David had just collected four faults at the wall.

This seemed to sober him down, and he pulled himself together and finished the course without any more faults.

" He *was* a fool," said John bitterly. " He needn't have crashed the wall."

The next two competitors both had refusals ; then there were several indifferent rounds. Alec, who was one of our hopes, proved to be simply awful. It was painful to watch him when we knew he could have jumped the course with his eyes shut if he'd only kept his head. He was horribly nervous and of course that made his pony nervous too. He got fourteen faults and rode off with his head down.

" There's still Hilda Marshall of ours," said Ann cheerfully. " You never know."

" Hilda Marshall ! " said John ironically. However to our surprise Hilda rode in as cool as a cucumber on Pretty Pete, her neat pigtails hardly swinging, and popped round the course as she had never popped round it during practices. She only collected two faults.

" Gosh ! " I said. " She might even be third. Wonders never cease."

" She could easily be third," said Ann excitedly. " All the funny people are winning everything today."

However there was another clear round by an outsider, and then somebody else besides Hilda got two faults.

The three clear round people jumped it off, and Betty Prince won. That settled the first, second, and third. Hilda and the other girl who had got two faults then jumped it off for fourth place, but Hilda's luck didn't hold and the other girl was much more experienced. Hilda got six faults over the three selected jumps and the other girl only two.

" So that's the junior jumping ! " I said. " Not one of our members in the first four. Isn't it murder ! "

We all said, " Bad luck, jolly well tried," to Hilda as she came off. The jumps were raised for the seniors.

" Isn't it grim ? " I said to Ann. " I've got the needle much worse than I ever had it at Chatton Show."

" Oh, don't let's think about those wretched juniors," said Ann. " It was just bad luck on the riding club, because both David and Alec could have done clear rounds if they'd been more careful. Let's ride as if we couldn't care less."

" I'd love to be in the first three myself," I said, " but honestly, in my present frame of mind I don't care who wins so long as it's a member of the riding club."

" Well, we've got a terrific chance," said Ann. " I mean, look at John—and Val—and Diana—and even Clarissa, quite apart from you and me. There's only really Helen Batterby and Judy Trowt and Peter Wishart to beat, and they've all been beaten by our crowd before. Come on. Up the Riding Club ! "

I suddenly felt frightfully cheerful and contented. It was pretty hopeful that at least *one* of us would be in the first three.

I rode Rapide round the jumps and he looked confident and felt very steady. He was always a very reassuring pony to ride, because he showed me clearly what he was feeling and I could understand him.

Clarissa Dandleby rode first. Some people hated riding first, but Clarissa said she didn't care. She held

her pony back so tightly that his canter between the
jumps wasn't much more than a collected walk, and
jumped from what was practically a standstill in a very
correct and uninspired way.   I could see the judges
frowning, but Clarissa only got two faults and rode out
in a very business-like way.

The next competitor, not one of us, got three refusals
at the first fence ; then Judy Trowt rode and had awfully
bad luck as her pony shied at something in the crowd,
reared and put her down.   The next few competitors
got about four or six faults each.   My cousin Cecilia
was warned by the judge for whacking her pony and
this annoyed her so much that she let herself be put off,
and got eight faults.

John Watson did a beautiful clear round ; so did
Val Heath.   I felt I didn't care now, as it was fairly
certain that unless there were an awful lot more clear
rounds we should have one or more of our members in
the first three.

Ann was unlucky and got six faults.   Peter Wishart
—one of those I feared—got a clear round.   Diana Bush,
one of our best, for some unknown reason got three
refusals at the last jump, the triple bar, and went out
looking very disappointed.   Helen Batterby, who told
us before she started that she had a strained leg and
was disobeying the doctor and her parents in coming at
all, had to retire at the third jump.

As I rode into the ring I summed up the situation.
There were already three clear rounds, John Watson,
Val Heath, and Peter Wishart.   There might still be
another or two from non-riding-club members.   A lot
depended on me still.   As I gathered Rapide for the
first jump the light but firm pressure of my hands told

him that this round was frightfully important, and a slight quiver of his satiny shoulder told me that he understood.

He took the brush fence so neatly that I hardly realised we were over, and without checking went competently over the next three. I helped him with the next one, the wall, for I knew it was his least-liked jump, and he obeyed beautifully. I had an instant of heart-failure at the gate, for I thought he had taken off a fraction too soon, but it was all right. Now for the triple bar. He was cooler than I, as if to say, it's okay this time.

Over we went, and I had never been so thrilled in my life as when I was riding out and patting Rapide while the spectators clapped our clear round.

" Jolly good ! " said Ann. " Oh, terrifically good ! " John Watson and Val also thumped me on the back, and we three stood waiting to see if there would be any more clear rounds. If not, it meant that the riding club would get three of the four prizes. But there *were* two more clear rounds, one of them by a very smart boy on a blood pony, and the other by—of all people on earth—April Cholly-Sawcutt !

We just couldn't believe it. Nobody could. We were stunned. April came out of the ring shrieking at the top of her voice that she had never jumped a clear round before in her life and she had simply kept her eyes shut all the time. Her father was standing there looking very pale and saying, " Hold me up, somebody. It isn't true." And the rest of us were thumping April on the back until she yelled for mercy.

" Six clear rounds ! " said John. " Six to jump off, four of ours and two outsiders. April, you were terrific.

Now you've got to shut your eyes, go into a trance, and do it again."

" I can't, I can't," wailed April. " I shall crash everything, like I always do."

" If you get into the last four," said her father, " I'll buy you the finest racing-model bike in Ryechester, I swear I will." I had never seen him so excited, in spite of his own great international successes. I knew it had been his life's greatest trial that his daughters were such utterly dud riders, and now to have two of them shine like stars on one day was too much joy.

At last the judges announced, " The six competitors who jumped clear rounds will now jump again. First, number 23."

This was Peter Wishart. The three selected jumps were the wall, the gate, and the triple. Peter's pony took the wall and the gate in a rather too dashing way, and then steadied for the triple.

" Oh, I hope he brings it down ! " breathed Ann, and John said, " Don't be so beastly unsporting," though I'm sure he felt the same as Ann.

The triple had been widened, and it was unlucky for Peter that he was riding first, for he took off too far away, jumped short, and brought down the farthest bar. The crowd groaned, and we were all sporting enough to call out, " Bad luck ! " instead of Hurrah. Peter had four faults.

" You next, John," I breathed, as his number was called. I knew in my heart that John was going to be all right because his pony looked so confident and was obviously dying to do the jumps again. To see her whisk over the wall and the gate was lovely, and she came up to the triple as if it was the easiest thing in the world. John went over like a bird, and the crowd clapped and cheered like mad.

Val rode next and got two faults by hitting the gate with her pony's forelegs. Then the smart boy, whose name was Barry Noble, went in and had awfully bad luck because his pony was over-heated and refused to jump at all.

" It's really his own fault," said John. " I noticed that he was too lazy to unsaddle and rest his pony while he was waiting and now he has to pay for it."

Next it was April's turn. None of us could bear to look. We expected nearly anything to happen. If April had stood on her head in the saddle I don't think anybody would have been surprised. But it certainly was her day. I saw her take the first jump with her eyes tightly shut. At the wall she got two faults, looked back, and yelled " Murder ! " at the top of her voice. Then off she went for the triple like a steam engine and we all covered our ears not to hear the crash.

There was no crash, only the sweet landing of hoofs on turf, and the next minute there was April riding off, grinning all over her face.

" Only two faults," she said. " You thought I couldn't do it. Shucks to you ! "

I will not go into details, but will only say that I did the three jumps with no faults. So there were John and I with no faults and Val and April with two each. The judge asked us what we would like to do.

We went into a huddle together, and then announced that we thought the ponies had had enough, and we had agreed to divide the first prize between John and me and the third between Val and April. John and I each got a red rosette and Val and April a yellow one.

It was beyond our wildest dreams that the riding club should have won all four places in the senior jumping, and when we rode round the ring with our rosettes the cheering could be heard for miles away, led by Captain Cholly-Sawcutt.   April was in tears by now, she was so thrilled, and she finished up by falling off her pony and

sitting on the ground with her legs stuck out in front of her, roaring her head off.

Even Clarissa came up to me and said very decently, " Congratulations, Jill. Nobody can say now that the riding school isn't the tops. And I heard Captain Cholly-Sawcutt telling your mother that anything less than a horsy career for you would be a crime."

I was so pleased I said, " Oh thanks, Clarissa. And it was jolly hard luck that you didn't get a clear round, because you deserved to."

By now the jumps were being cleared away, and it was the Gretna Green Race. The seniors' names were put into one tin and the juniors into another. We all prayed we should get a nice light-weight " bride," but of course I had to go and draw Stanley Trimble who was as big as I was ! Ann was worse off still as she drew a very solid little girl called Meg North, who looked as if it would take a crane to get her off the ground. Peter Wishart was the luckiest as he drew Pam Derry who was very small and light, and Clarissa said, " Just my luck ! I did hope I'd win *something*, and this was my last chance, and I've got June Cholly-Sawcutt who weighs a ton."

We all mounted and went thundering down the course at a mad gallop to where the " brides " were waiting. Peter Wishart was miles ahead, it looked as if he only had to sweep little Pam up and be home long before anybody else.

As I struggled to heave Stanley up behind me on Black Boy I saw Ann and Meg North flat on the ground, and just beyond them was Peter looking wildly at Pam. He had swung down impatiently and lost his reins, and his pony, thinking this was part of the game, had cantered away. I hadn't time to see what happened next, Stanley was up behind me and I was trying to convince Black Boy that he enjoyed the double load.

To my surprise I saw Clarissa, cool and unbothered, with fat little June already clasping her waist and the pony behaving beautifully. They were off, and about a dozen of us pounding after. One or two of the " brides " were practically upside down and clutching on fiercely. Val Heath was in the lead but she didn't keep it for long ; Peter Wishart had recaptured his pony, whisked Pam up, and was off in hot pursuit.

But now it looked as if Clarissa was in front. A crowd of us crossed the winning line in a bunch, and as we pulled up the " brides " flew off in all directions.

Clarissa, in spite of the weight, had won, and Peter Wishart in a furious gallop had come in second. Amid clapping the rosettes were given out.

I thumped Clarissa on the back and said, " You were terrific, and I hope you get a jolly good prize for that effort."

With surprising modesty she said that she had under-rated June, who instead of being a dead loss had kicked Havelock in the right spot at the right moment and so shot home.

We thought everything was now over and that the ponies and we ourselves would have time to cool down before the prizes were given, but Cecilia came up and said, " What do you think ? This will slay you. Miss Durdon says that all the members of the riding club have to tidy up quickly and do a grand march past."

" Oh no ! " I gasped.

" That's what she says."

Hurriedly we rubbed the ponies down and tried to make ourselves look presentable, which wasn't easy. I tidied Ann's hair and she tidied mine, as we hadn't a mirror, and we straightened each other's ties, and that was about all we could do.

Miss Durdon, resplendent in hunting kit, was waiting. She had even got a rose in her buttonhole. We all lined up behind her, the younger ones in front and we big ones at the back, and slowly rode round the ring, blushing madly when people cheered. I caught the eye of Major Hooley who was muttering something about, "Legs! Legs!" Then he turned to the man next to him and talked very earnestly. Doubtless telling what a time he had had with us.

It suddenly occurred to me that people had something to clap about. The riding club was riding very well indeed, with straight backs, hands down, knees up, and cool but conscious pride on their faces. They looked good. They looked wonderful. They really were something to shout about and I felt frightfully happy.

Behind Miss Durdon we went twice round the ring. Then she dismissed the parade and disappeared into the judges' tent, only to emerge about five minutes later to present the prizes. She was completely transformed, having somehow managed to get out of her riding clothes and into a very fashionable rig-out of pink, with beads and a floppy hat, and gloves.

The numerous and smashing prizes took every eye. John Watson and I had to share the silver cup for the senior jumping, so we decided to have it for six months each in turn, and he very sportingly insisted that I should have it first which gave me the privilege of carrying it off the field. The silver stirrups we had so much admired went to Betty Prince, who wasn't in the riding club, but she deserved them.

Stanley Trimble won Mrs. Darcy's box of stable equipment and nearly forgot himself so far as to whoop for joy, but managed to turn it into a cough. All the other winners got useful things like ties and brushes and boxes of chocolates, and Mercy got a martingale as Miss Durdon's special prize and didn't know what it was for! She stood looking at it in a helpless kind of way, and said to John Watson, " Which end of the pony does it go on ? "

The three Cholly-Sawcutt girls all got prizes, which nearly rendered their father unconscious. One felt it was the sort of thing that could never happen again in the history of the world. June got a box of chocolates

for being the winning " bride," and within one minute had the lid off and was passing them round the judges ! This wasn't conventional, but everybody was rather pleased and thought it quite a gesture for June.

Then Major Hooley worked his way to the front and made a speech which I couldn't hear, and somebody

called for three cheers for the judges. After that Miss
Durdon called for three cheers for everybody who had
worked so hard to make the gymkhana a success, and
we realised it was all over.

Major Hooley came up to me and solemnly shook
hands, saying, " I didn't think you people had it in you
but I was mistaken. I congratulate you on what you've
achieved." Which I thought was very nice of him.

Some of us stayed behind to help to clear up.

" I must say, I think this gymkhana has been the
most fun of anything I've been to this summer," said
Ann.

" I think the riding club has been the best fun of
anything I've ever done," said David Neville.

" I seem to have learnt a lot from it," said Val Heath.

Stanley Trimble said he really didn't see how the
seniors could have learnt anything as they had been
teaching the juniors all the time.

" I expect what we've learnt is how to teach," I said.
" That's a good thing."

" And how not to be cocksure about ourselves," said
John Watson.

" And how to share things with the younger ones and
not think we were the tops all the time," said Ann.

" Well, that's the whole point of a riding club," I
said. " We shan't know till tomorrow how much money
the gymkhana has made, but it must be a lot, and we
hadn't a great many expenses so the animal charities
will do well."

" At least," said John Watson, " our parents won't
be able to say, ' It'll be a good thing when you go back
to school, you never find anything useful to do in the
holidays.' "

" On the contrary," said Clarissa, " they ought to give us a pat on the back."

We finished clearing away and the rays of the sinking sun turned the grass to gold while long shadows of trees crept over the lane.

" So the sordid shadows of school fall on the riding club," I said poetically. " But it was awfully good while it lasted."